Heaven and Beyond

A NOVEL

Michael Phillips

ABOUT THE AUTHOR

Michael Phillips is a novelist, biblical scholar, historian, and devotional writer whose books have been embraced by readers around the world. His nonfiction books include biographies of Victorian author George MacDonald and Olympic athlete-turned-Congressman Jim Ryun. In the 1980s, Phillips' edited and facsimile editions of MacDonald's near-forgotten works inspired a worldwide resurgence of interest in the Scotsman whose writing helped inspire C.S. Lewis' conversion from atheism to Christianity. Over the years Phillips has come to be recognized as a man with keen insight into MacDonald's understanding of God's heart of Fatherhood.

Phillips is best known for his fiction, a corpus that includes sixty titles, encompassing beloved historical novels set throughout the world.

As his own volume of work reaches a stature of significance in its own right, Phillips is regarded, like Lewis before him, as one of many successors to George MacDonald's vision and spiritual legacy for a new generation.

More information about Michael Phillips, and a complete list of his books, can be found at Wikipedia or FatherOfTheInklings.com.

Heaven and Beyond: A Novel
Copyright © 2015 by Michael Phillips

First edition 2015 by Yellowood House, an imprint of Sunrise Books

ISBN: 9780940652453

PREFACE

This is a work of fiction. I make no claim to have had a "vision of heaven" or anything resembling it. I do not present this story as a theological treatise, still less as predictive of what anyone may or may not experience in the next life. It is a "story" which I hope will be meaningful in unique ways to those who read it.

My emphasis on this as imaginative fiction, however, does not diminish the fact that I have also written what follows to stimulate our thoughts, perhaps prompt discussion, and in the Apostle Paul's words to "widen our hearts." George MacDonald speaks often of the vital role the imagination plays in helping us know God and his ways. As C.S. Lewis says in the preface to his classic *The Great Divorce*, we do not and cannot know what the afterlife holds. Yet our imaginations have been created by God to point us toward him.

This being so, it has seemed to me that drawing upon a wide range of what Lewis calls "imaginative supposals" will guard against imbalance or over-emphasis on any one theme, and may in the end "widen our hearts" to possibilities awaiting us in heaven. As I have done so in this fictitious glimpse of the future, I should make clear that the narrator in what follows is not intended to represent a specific likeness of *me* any more than do the atheist and the gardener in the companion volumes of this trilogy. Hopefully readers will find *themselves* in these pages more than they find me. This is an imaginative fantasy and should be read in that light.

Mostly it is my desire to give hope to both the living and the dying—hope to believe the eternal truth expressed by George MacDonald's brother on his deathbed, that "this is nae the end o' it." If this little story can encourage a few souls to anticipate the transition out of this life into more Life with greater faith, renewed hope, even joy, I will have succeeded in what I set out to do. As for the rest, borrowing from MacDonald himself, I hope you will enjoy it "for the tale."

Michael Phillips

THE BEYOND TRILOGY
by Michael Phillips

The Garden at the Edge of Beyond
Heaven and Beyond
Hell and Beyond

Contents

Preface

In my Father's house are many mansions; if it were not so, would I have told you that I go to prepare a place for you? And when I go and prepare a place for you, I will come again and take you to myself, that where I am you may be also.

A little while, and you will see me no more; again a little while…I will see you again and your hearts will rejoice, and no one will take your joy from you.

ONE

Easter Reflections

The morning dawned crisp and bright. It was the perfect prelude to a glorious Easter sunrise.

My wife and I had talked about attending a sunrise service. After the previous evening commemorating our anniversary, however, we decided to satisfy ourselves with the eleven o'clock service.

A thin mist spread across the hills in the distance, evidence of the night's lingering chill on this early April morning. The day would warm and the mist burn off. Spring fragrances filled the air. New life was sprouting up and budding out. The earth proclaimed the message of Easter everywhere, though most of its inhabitants remained unseeing and unhearing of those wondrous tidings.

Nothing in the appearance of the morning boded singular significance as heralding a day that would change my life forever...literally.

I had been working the previous afternoon in the small enclosed yard behind our home. The pleasure of gardening had always been for me an extension of my spiritual life. I loved growing things—whether people or plants. Space was limited in our senior community, however. Houses and gardens were small. But I cultivated a few plants of special meaning, both as reminders of larger gardens in previous homes, as well as for their deeper significance. At one end we had also added a water feature, with a small stream tumbling over two small waterfalls and through rocks down a three foot high hill into a tiny pond at its base.

With Spring coming on, though the main pruning had already been done, I had been giving special attention to several grapevines and five prized roses. Both species were favorites as daily examples of God's creative hand in the universe, and his work in the hearts of his men and women.

I loved vines as vivid images of the Lord's description in John 15 of humanity's intricate shared relationship with Father and Son. And I loved roses as living representations of God's purpose in human life—to grow each of us into the unique perfection, or *blossom*, of our being. My favorite author, an old Victorian Scotsman, had expressed this last truth in the colorful words:

"Who but a father could think the flowers for his little ones?

"The truth of the flower is not the facts about it, but the shining, glowing, gladdening, patient thing throned on its stalk—the compeller of smile and tear from child and prophet.

"Here is a truth of nature, the truth of a flower—a truth of God! A man's likeness to Christ is the truth of a man, in the same way that the perfect meaning of a flower is the truth of a flower. The truth of every man is the perfected Christ in him. As Christ is the blossom of humanity, so the blossom of every man is the Christ perfected in him."

I never gazed upon the blossom of a *Peace, Secret,* or *Sunsprite* without thinking that God was also growing *me* into just such a blossom in *his* eternal garden.

The evening before my wife and I had been more than usually reflective on our life together. Birthdays and anniversaries tend to do that the more rapidly life progresses. The changes of life brought on by advancing age, the passing of our parents, and watching our children grow older, all took on the luster of greater significance now that we were both in our eighth decade. We ordered Chinese take-out and watched *Swing Time,* our favorite Astaire and Rogers movie. Then we talked late into the evening, sharing fond memories of times past, and wondering what the future might still have for us.

It was a special anniversary. The evening represented only the third time since our wedding fifty-two years earlier that was followed the next day by Easter. We had planned our wedding for the Saturday before Easter, not realizing what a rarity it would prove to be to celebrate both notable occasions on the same weekend.

Now I was up early, as was my custom, awaiting the Easter sunrise. The air was still. The sun had just begun to creep above the eastern horizon. I was conscious of a deeper quiet than usual, a peace overspreading the damp feathery haze that hovered over the foothills at the edge of town. The peace was not merely external like the mist, but internal. My heart was serene. Something seemed at hand.

Heavy drops hung from the tiny delicate leaves emerging throughout our small garden. I marveled again that God could produce such infinite variations of beauty out of the soil of the ground. I envisioned the roots and leaves drawing precious dew from earth and air, unseen by the eye, which was transformed through their stalks and vines by the wonder of that "natural" process we call *growth*—which is in truth a miracle of stupendous supernatural power and significance—into tiny succulent grapes or the spectacular colors and fragrances of a *Double Delight* or *Mr. Lincoln* rose.

What glories the coming Spring and Summer would produce. The very thought of the burgeoning growth of the plants around me, what they were *becoming*, filled my heart with joy.

I retrieved my clippers and proceeded slowly among the vines. Here and there I plucked or trimmed an errant shoot so that the blood of the vine might flow up the main trunk, reflecting that the miracle of both grapes and roses was not one of mere natural law, but of spiritual truth.

I thought how my life, too, might be likened to these plants I nurtured. And I considered again the ancient words:

"I am the true vine, and my Father is the vinedresser. As the branch cannot bear fruit by itself, unless it abides in the vine, neither can you, unless you abide in me. I am the vine, you are the branches. He who abides in me, and I in him, he it is that bears much fruit. As the Father has loved me, so have I loved you; abide in my love."

My thoughts stilled yet more. My heart drifted toward introspective prayer.

Prune from within me, heavenly Vinedresser, I whispered, *those branches that are not bearing heavenly fruit. Graft me more fully into the vine of your eternal being, that I might bear your fruit in my character. Show me what heaven is like, so that I can live in its reality here and now. May I live eternally in you, now and forever.*

After making my way about our yard, my heart full of many things, I turned back inside. It was time to put on the water for coffee and tea.

Two

Thunderbolt From A Clear Sky

In the house a short time later, my wife and I picked up our reminiscing where we had left off the night before. We continued nostalgic as we enjoyed our morning coffee and tea together, reading and talking quietly.

In spite of hardships, heartbreaks, and the endemic pains and disappointments of life, we were grateful to the Lord and one another for the years we had enjoyed. I was seventy-six, she seventy-four. We were in good health and looking forward to many anniversaries to come.

Were our contemplative musings perhaps a premonition, or merely the result of passing another of life's yearly milestones? If they were in some way a foreshadowing, we were certainly unaware of it.

Yet...life is fleeting. Some changes flow into the rivers of our lives gradually. Others shock the system with sudden unpredictability. Death itself, though expected and inevitable in one sense, never arrives as one anticipates. Some perhaps have opportunity to prepare for it while battling cancer, some other debilitating illness, or simply during the long decline of age. For victims of strokes, heart attacks, or accidents, however, the end often comes so suddenly there is no time to put the past in order.

However it comes—whether to the thirty year old or the centenarian—in another way no one is really ever prepared. We put off thinking about it. In a sense, the *cause* of death hardly matters. Death is the great equalizer which renders all causes, illnesses, accidents, and terminal conditions meaningless. Standing before the door of beyond, we all arrive naked and empty-handed.

If I may be permitted to quote the Scotsman again, my old literary friend described the abruptness of life's changes in this way:

"Sometimes a thunderbolt will shoot from a clear sky; and sometimes into the life of a peaceful individual, without warning of gathered storm, something terrible will fall. And from that moment everything is changed. That life is no more what it was. Forever after, its spiritual weather is altered. But for the one who believes in God, such rending and frightful catastrophes never come but where they are turned around for good in his own life and in other lives he touches."

Such a thunderbolt was gathering on the horizon of our lives. It was moving toward us rapidly. But we saw no sign of its approach.

Our morning passed quietly. We were in the car on our way to church by 10:15. Anticipating a large Easter turnout, our pastor had encouraged as many as possible to attend at nine. However, we were old school, one might say. We did not enjoy the new trends in church music. We preferred the more traditional environment and familiar hymns of the eleven o'clock service. We thus made our plans accordingly.

There had been reports on the news of potential incidents. Several cities were said to be targeted for high-profile reprisals against what extremists called "the evils of Christianity." Our city happened to be one of them.

Yet one always takes such warnings with a grain of salt. After all, what are the odds? The danger will never come close.

The church parking lot was crowded when we pulled in about 10:30. Cars from the early service and Sunday school were leaving as new arrivals poured into north and south entrances.

We parked, got out, and walked hand in hand toward the church building, greeting friends as we went.

I glanced at my wife beside me, radiant with her trademark smile. My heart filled again with love for this woman God had chosen for me to spend my life with. She was positively beautiful in my eyes. The crown of white on her head was a resplendent tiara of character, fit symbol of a life spent as a growing daughter of God.

Walking amid a group of ten or fifteen from the lot, we neared the church building talking and visiting together.

I glanced beyond the adjacent street. The church sat across from several high rise apartment buildings. Nothing in particular drew my eye. I simply moved my head unconsciously in that direction.

A brilliant flash suddenly exploded from one of the buildings. It was followed by a second, then a third.

I heard nothing. I was only aware the next instant of a terrific blow slamming into my chest. I thought I had been bludgeoned with a sledgehammer.

My senses went into slow-motion. My first thought was heart attack.

All around people were running frantically. I saw their mouths shouting and screaming. But I could not hear them. I could not run with them. My feet were cemented to the ground.

My vision blurred. I felt neither hands nor feet.

I turned toward my wife. She was clutching at me. Her eyes filled with panic and terror.

I felt myself going faint. My knees buckled.

Then blackness engulfed me.

THREE

Coming to Terms

It did not take long after groggily coming to myself before the realization became stark and clear: I would not recover.

I knew I was dying.

Everything I had been reflecting on about life had come upon me more suddenly than I could have imagined. Had my Easter morning thoughts and prayers been a harbinger of my own impending death?

It hardly mattered. I was lying in a hospital bed with tubes attached all over me and coming out of my nose and mouth, and with monitors beeping around me. I was utterly motionless, unable to move a little finger.

Worse, I was completely incapable of communicating with the outside world. I could tell that my body had been shattered beyond repair. It was time to turn the earthly tabernacle in on a new model.

My recollections of the incident were hazy. I had felt nothing, and felt nothing much now other than motionlessness, helplessness, and the vague discomfort of things tugging at various parts of my body. I still assumed I had suffered a heart attack. My first thought was for my wife. I tried to open my eyes and look about. I must be paralyzed, I thought. I couldn't move even my eyelids. That's when I began to think that something more than a heart attack might be going on.

Instinctively I knew that recovery was out of the question. I was probably lucky to be alive at all, even—which seemed clearly my status—if only on life support.

I had lived a long life. I was ready to go. This wasn't how I'd envisioned it—though who ever dies according to plan? Death is the supreme *un*planned event of life. But I was not afraid of death.

Being ready to die didn't mean I wasn't full of protest. I faced the normal initial reactions—the frustration of suddenly finding myself so helpless, the complaints stirred up in my mind against the "unfairness" of it all, the dozens of ways the question *Why me?* rears its head, as if anyone ever promised that life was supposed to be fair.

So many thoughts, too, revolved around my dear wife. My whole being ached for what she must be going through. And for this to have happened on Easter Sunday…I hoped this wouldn't forever after spoil our anniversary and Easter for her.

Such thoughts suddenly brought to mind the question how long I had been here. Was it the day after Easter, or a week later…even a month?

I had no idea how long I had been lying in this room, or if perhaps my wife had also been injured in whatever had happened.

Was she in the bed next to me…or, worse, might she even have been killed?

Pervading the turbulence of speculation that comes at such a time was the despondency that floods one's soul to realize that life as you know it is over.

Gradually, however, I got over those responses and determined to make the best of it.

An old 17th century prayer was burned into my mind from years of seeing it framed on a wall in our home. A few of its words now returned probingly to my mind: *Keep me reasonably sweet. I do not want to be a saint—some of them are so hard to live with. But a sour old person is one of the crowning works of the devil. Give me the ability to see good things in unexpected places...*

Okay, I thought, it was time to practice what I preached. It was time to see if I could approach death with grace, dignity, sweetness, and without complaint. I was old. This had happened. I loathed the very thought of becoming a *sour* old person. What an awful way to exit life. Even if my comatose state prevented me voicing irritation and complaint aloud, I didn't want to become sour even to myself. However long I had— hours, days, weeks...whatever—I *would* be kind-hearted and sweet, even if only within the silence of my own mind.

Once I came to terms with the inevitable fact that I was not going to recover, along with my determination to face death bravely and sweetly, I began looking forward to it. So many questions and perplexities and theological conundrums would soon be answered. A great adventure awaited me!

I suppose if I were brutally honest I would have to confess to being just a *little* nervous. Not afraid of the idea of death. But uneasy about the process of dying itself, and what I would find as I walked through that unknown door.

Would it hurt? Would I be aware of what was happening? Would I still be *me*?

Then there was the whole nebulous idea of "heaven." Christians talk and sing about it. But when it comes down to it, heaven is a greater unknown than death itself.

I wasn't worried about where I would spend eternity. Yet no matter how strong one's faith, who is not curiously apprehensive about what death and heaven will actually be like?

How many of my preconceptions about the afterlife would turn out to be true?

What would be different than expected? What might I have been wrong about?

How much reality would I discover there had been in the many highly-publicized "visions" of heaven and hell? Had they been true visions, hoaxes, innocent delusions...or perhaps just dreams?

Would I even be allowed to see hell?

How old would I be?

Would I know family and friends?

What would time be like in a place where a day was as a thousand years, and a thousand years as a day?

And in the words of the old children's book I had read so often to my sons, what would people in heaven *do* all day?

On top of these were the myriad theologic uncertainties that made up the list of things I wanted to "ask God some day." They were completely diverse: Where did Cain's wife come from...how long did creation take...how much about evolution was true...who wrote *Hebrews*...was Noah's ark still intact on the earth...did life exist elsewhere in the heavens...were Adam and Eve real people...how did God create matter out of nothingness...how did he set off the Big Bang...what were the true entry requirements for heaven?

Or would all such conundrums vanish from my mind the instant I crossed the threshold?

It surprised me that more people didn't talk about their thoughts and hopes and uncertainties. Through the years as a hospital and hospice volunteer, I'd sat at the bedside of countless men and women as death approached. But no one spoke of it.

FOUR

Bucket Lists

It may sound strange that I was contemplating such things. But just laying on my back…waiting… drifting in and out of consciousness…I could do nothing else *but* think. All I had left was my mind.

My greatest regret was leaving my wife. But we had passed the fifty year mark together two years before. Maybe it was time to say good-bye. Again, not like I'd planned. There was so much I wanted to say to the one who had shared life with me. Now that my tongue was stilled, however, I had to let the memories speak for me.

As my first hours of silent awareness passed, with the relief of hearing my wife's voice in the room speaking occasionally with nurses, I learned that it was now four days after Easter, and that a shooting had taken place outside our church.

Apparently the incident was big news, though I was the only serious casualty.

We had tried to think of different scenarios that might occur as we aged—strokes, Alzheimer's, loss of mobility. We had even tried to devise plans how to communicate if one of us became incapable of speech.

But we hadn't thought of a coma. I suppose as prepared for death as you try to be, or think you are, you can never *really* prepare for the unforeseen and unknown.

My poor wife's tearful words as she sat at my bedside were a daily anguish. That was another reason I was anxious to go. Long good-byes are always uncomfortable. I hoped this one wouldn't drag on longer than necessary.

She would grieve. However, she was a strong and resolute woman. She would be fine. She had already lost the me she knew anyway. I could hear her when she spoke to me, and feel her touch as she held my limp hand. It broke my heart to listen. I knew she had no idea whether I could hear her or not. I was in what the doctors called a "deep coma." Now that my brain had woken up, however, I heard every word. At least she didn't talk baby talk like several of the nurses. She spoke to me in the same voice she always had. I was grateful for that. I felt awake, that I ought to be able to converse with her. Yet my body was incapable of response.

In the minds of the doctors who came and went, I was already dead. They were trying to find a gracious way to persuade my wife, as they called it when she wasn't listening, to let them "pull the plug."

Hey, wait a minute! I wanted to shout. *I'm not dead yet. Don't put that on her.*

I was ready for *God* to pull the plug. But no wife ought to be forced into such an agonizing decision. Death should be a peaceful transition, not a heart-wrenching series of impossible choices.

How desperately I longed for a way to reassure my wife that I was okay, that I was at peace, that my bodily pain was no more than I could bear, and that I was looking forward to whatever came next.

All I could do was lie there. I hoped that somehow my brain waves might connect with hers in such a way that she could share my peace. We had always talked about the ESP that sometimes seemed to flow between us. I needed that ESP to work especially hard right now.

We had been talking about our so-called bucket lists for years. We'd done our best to prepare ourselves for the end of life by making sure we had no relational "issues" hanging around. If we needed to forgive or to ask forgiveness for insensitivities or hurts we had caused, we had tried to deal with them. There were a few relationships, we realized, that would have to wait for the other side to be healed. But mostly the relational slates between the two of us were as clean as we were capable of making them.

We hadn't traveled widely. We'd seen all we desired to see of the world. When people spoke of bucket lists, those lists usually contained places they wanted to go, and perhaps people they wanted to meet. Our bucket lists had little to do with vacations or sightseeing. We had never been on a cruise. We had not visited Hawaii, New Zealand, Russia, Alaska, Japan or a thousand other places…and had no desire to.

We had been to Scotland several times. Our souls resonated with nature, history, and life's spiritual themes when we were there. That ancient land fulfilled our travel ambitions.

Our bucket lists, therefore, were more personal. They concerned the man and woman we wanted to become, changes we wanted to make within ourselves before death overtook us and we were left with whatever qualities of character we had allowed to be built into our souls.

There were people I wanted to meet, of course. But all of them were dead already—mentors, relatives, authors, my parents, Peter and Paul, the gospelist Mark. Meeting them, therefore, would not qualify for a bucket list. It was rather something I was eagerly waiting for on the other side.

I had a million questions I wanted to ask all those departed people too.

FIVE

The Harp

In the midst of my reflections, I became aware of subdued voices.

A woman was talking quietly to my wife. If I heard correctly, she was asking if she might play for me. I gathered that she was a musician visiting patient rooms.

"That would be nice," I heard my wife say.

"Though he won't hear you. He's on life support."

"Don't be too sure," said the lady. "Music has a remarkable capacity to get inside the heart and brain in ways we are unaware of."

"Whether he does or not, I will enjoy it. It has been a long few days."

Wait! I wanted to shout. *I can hear. And yes, I would like the music too.*

The woman was speaking again. It was almost as if she heard my silent plea.

"Music is always looking for secret ways inside," she said. "I call them back doors of consciousness. Music probes and penetrates and touches deeper internal chords than we realize. Even the vibrations of the harp strings exert a healing and soothing influence."

The *harp* strings, I thought. The lady was a harpist! The word sent a thrill of happiness through me.

I'm not sure how calming it would have been had a clarinetist or trumpet player walked into the room. But I felt my body relaxing at the mere *thought* of a harp.

Though I could not see her face, and probably never would, I knew that God had led this lady to my room. She had been sent to prepare me for what was coming, to bring peace not only to me but to my wife. The harp was the perfect confirmation that heaven was waiting, that God was good...and that all was well.

"Is your husband...he *is* your husband?" the harp lady was saying.

"Yes—we've been married fifty two years."

"That's wonderful. Congratulations. Not many couples can say that. How is he doing?"

"As well as can be expected, I suppose. He is not expected to recover."

"Oh, I am sorry. What happened—a heart attack, or—"

"No, he was strong and fit. There was an accident. Actually, he was shot."

"Goodness—that's awful. He's not the man shot by that terrorist at the church on Easter?"

"Yes, actually he is."

"Oh, my! I heard about it on the news. I am *so* sorry!"

"We were innocent bystanders, as they say. We were at the wrong place at the wrong time. We were just going into church. My husband happened to be the one who was hit. The instant we heard the shots, I felt him slump. Seconds later he collapsed on top of me."

"How frightening. I saw the policemen in the corridor. Are they to do with the shooting?"

"They don't think it was random. They questioned me yesterday. They're hoping my husband wakes up so they can talk to him. I told them he won't be waking up. There is no possible connection between us and the terrorist. But they insist that their investigation must leave no stone unturned in searching for him."

"He got away?"

"Yes. But it hardly matters now—at least to us. I wish the police would just leave it alone. Whoever he is, the man is in God's hands now."

"I will certainly keep you both in my prayers. Now I think perhaps I should play."

I heard a slight movement and rustling. Then the music began. It started so slowly and quietly that it seemed it had always been there.

It was beyond anything I could have dared hope for. I didn't actually hear singing. Yet I sensed that angels were nearby.

The sound of the harp strings transported me out of the isolation of my thoughts. Suddenly heaven invaded the hospital room and took over my soul.

How can I describe the *music* itself, the harmonies and arpeggios and chord progressions…the melancholy strains that made me ache with pleasant nostalgia, the joyful hymns that made my heart soar?

The harpist played in a soft continuous succession of melodies, transitioning from one to the other so seamlessly that I could hardly tell when one song ended and another began.

She began with soothing background music. It wasn't long, however, before tunes began to emerge out of the nebulous progression of sounds. Sometimes I gradually recognized a bit of a melody, but then just as quickly it would flit away like a butterfly lifting off a flower into the sunshine.

Desperately I tried to sing along whenever I heard something familiar. My lips refused to budge. The instant I heard *I'll Fly Away,* my feet itched to tap out the beat. The music was so happy! I had to satisfy myself to singing and clapping and tapping in my mind.

In the midst of the nostalgic tunes of the past, now and then came one or another haunting refrain from Scotland's treasure trove of music that my wife and I loved—*Wild Mountain Thyme, Auld Lang Syne, Loch Lomond, Over the Sea to Skye.* Whoever this lady was, she knew Scotland!

Best of all were the hymns.

Oh, the hymns!

They filled me with such happiness, every one evoking more memories than it would be possible to describe! It reminded me of singing in church when I was a boy.

One after another they came…*Fairest Lord Jesus, Just As I Am, This is My Father's World, It is Well With My Soul, Be Thou My Vision, Amazing Grace, In the Garden*…and that wonderful hymn we had discovered in the old 12th century church in Scotland, *The Quiet Center.*

When she played *How Great Thou Art*—so slow and low that it matched the groanings of my heart—my spirit rejoiced.

Even the simple children's song *Jesus Loves Me* moved my heart to the profoundest depths. The moment I heard it, I began to cry.

Jesus loves *me*! Yes, Jesus loves *me*!

I don't know whether I was crying with real tears. So much of my physical body had shut down. But *inside* I was crying. I felt the healing tears washing me clean.

The great variety of music flowing from those wonderful strings—whole songs along with snatches of familiar melodies—had the effect of causing my life to sweep across the screen of my memory in the span of a few minutes.

I heard my wife gasp. "There are tears on his cheeks!" she whispered to the harp lady.

They were tears of happiness. I was in a world of my own...boyhood fun...childhood playmates... climbing the redwood trees near my home...camping trips...church services... youth camp in the Sierras...memorable college days... treasured friendships...dancing with my wife, one minute to a country waltz, the next swinging to Glenn Miller or the Beach Boys...growing contentedly old together. My heart filled with the joy of life.

Gradually the music softened, then slowed. It became quiet, soft, and slow. At length it stopped.

I heard the lady stand and take a few steps toward the bed. The next moment her hand took mine. She held it several moments. I knew she was praying for me.

"God bless you, dear man," she whispered. "Your faithful wife is here beside you and loves you so very much. God is with you, too. Be brave and courageous. You are loved."

Thank you for your music, I shouted silently. *I heard every note! It brought such peace. It means more than you realize.* I hoped the music had given my wife as much peace as it had me.

The harpist slipped her hand from mine and returned to her chair.

"I would like to play one more song for your husband," said the lady.

"Thank you," replied my wife softly. Then she added, "Your music felt like a massage for my soul. Thank you so much for coming in."

It was silent a moment, then the harpist began again. The haunting sounds of some new melody carried me far away. It was no tune I recognized. Yet it struck deep into my depths. Whatever the song was, I felt that it had been composed just for me.

The slow haunting strains pulled and tugged at my spirit. They transported me to a place I seemed once to have known…to a country of long-forgotten childhood, but even older than that. Wherever it was, the impressions were vaguely familiar, full of deep and meaningful nostalgia, now remembered anew as where I had always been meant to live.

A pang of longing seized me. It was the joyful yearning for a lost homeland. Hungry as I was to drink in the deliciously strange melodics and harmonics, I felt myself growing sleepy.

It was a deeper drowsiness than usual, and as curiously different as were the sensations roused by the spirit strings.

Six

A Waking

The sounds of the lady's unknown melody grew faint.

It did not occur to me at first that maybe I wasn't going to *sleep* at all. But it was exactly *like* going to sleep...warm, cozy...quiet...and so peaceful.

I was a child again, without a care in the world, drifting off in the back seat of the car knowing that my father was at the wheel and would still be there when I woke.

The music of the harp had taken me back to my childhood...and perhaps beyond it.

The quietness grew preternaturally deep. The monitors and distant sounds of the hospital faded. The music of the harp melted away. The unheard angel voices dissolved into the silence of beyond from whence they had come.

Silence. Only silence.

At last I was alone amid the deepest stillness I had ever known.

Finally I slept.

But my nap—if a nap it was—lasted only seconds.

An intense white light shocked me awake. I realized that my sight was working again. My eyelids twitched. I blinked a time or two from the brightness, still with my eyes closed, then slowly opened them.

For the first time I could see the hospital room that had been my home for several days. The harpist was still playing. My wife sat across the room, her head slumped back. The eerily moving melody had put her to sleep too.

I wanted to shout, *Hey, everybody—I'm awake!*

Still I had no voice. Come to think of it, I couldn't hear either. I was still enveloped in the deep silence. I saw the lady's fingers playing the strings. I felt their vibrations. But I heard nothing.

Another twitch came, this time to my arms. Then I was aware of my legs. Life was returning to my limbs!

Eager to be off my back, I sat up and swung my legs over the sides of the bed. Slowly I stood.

I felt great! Strong and alive again, full of energy.

I hadn't noticed in the first moments, but a door across the room led outside rather than into the hospital corridor. From what I could see, it opened into an expansive garden adjacent to the building. I'd heard one of the nurses mention a Healing Garden. That must be it, I thought. How convenient that my room sat right next to it. The door was open and bursting with sunlight.

The brilliance drew me. I left the room and walked outside.

Instantly I was assaulted not merely by light, but by the fragrances of the luxuriant garden filled with paths and flowers and tiny grassy oases of light. The pleasure was indescribable.

A sense of well-being and power surged through me. Brightness of pure luminescence engulfed me. The light was so full I wanted to taste it, drink it, eat it. It went *through* me, and *into* me with living, pulsating, throbbing, living *energy*.

Slowly I made my way through the vortex of light into the garden. It was larger than I had realized. In the distance I saw fields, valleys, and woodlands spreading in all directions. The city and hospital disappeared. I looked down to see that I was walking across a luxuriant grassy sward—a soft carpet of luscious green.

The air was warm and full. Its faint breeze carried on its wings the most unimaginable scents. Flowers sprang up everywhere. The aromas filled my head with fragrances unimaginable.

As I took in the sights and smells with wonder, I saw in the distance the figure of a man coming toward me.

I knew him instantly.

I cannot say how he was dressed. Neither can I describe the face that slowly emerged out of the light.

He came closer. What came next shocked me. He broke into a run, a great exuberant smile on his face. I ran to him, weeping great tears of joy.

He opened his arms wide as we met, then stopped and swallowed me in his embrace.

We stood for what seemed an eternity. Contentment is the only word to describe what I felt.

Calm.

Tranquility.

Rest.

Peace.

A hush as of the ages descended upon the universe. This was the moment Creation had been created for. Every moment of my life had pointed to this instant, this embrace, this homecoming.

All heaven seemed waiting breathlessly for what

would come next.

At last he spoke. His Voice softly filled the silence. The words came almost whispered in my ear:

"Well done!" he said. "Well *done*, my dear, dear friend! You have lived well. My Father and I are pleased. Welcome home! I have so looked forward to meeting you here."

"And I you," I replied. "Though you are not what I imagined."

"I never am!" he rejoined, chuckling as we stepped back. "But come—I have much to show you! Most of it will likewise be different than you expected, or would even have been capable of imagining. But my faithful ones catch on quickly to the new realities here."

I drew in a deep sigh. The air that filled my lungs was palpably rich with vitality.

"You will find that you have much to learn," he went on, "many new truths await. A journey of discovery more exciting than you envisioned in your wildest dreams lies before you. Heaven beckons! You will love it! But expect surprises and new revelations. The instant you see them, you will know them for the realities your heart always longed for."

He turned and led me along a new path further into the garden.

"Is this the hospital garden?" I asked.

"It is sometimes called the Garden at the Edge of Beyond."

"Will my wife be alright?"

"You and she were always alright. But yes, she will be fine. She will continue to grow. She is already yearning to follow you."

"Does everyone come here...first, I mean—after the white light?"

"All needs are not the same. All stories are

different. Everyone arrives where they need to be."

He smiled, then chuckled lightly again. "My, but you *are* a curious fellow!" he said.

"Sorry," I said sheepishly.

"Don't apologize. We like inquisitive minds here. But…Cain's wife!" he added, now laughing outright.

"It's something I've always wondered about."

"You and ten million others!"

"You knew what I was thinking…back there?"

"Of course. Nothing new under the sun, as they say. I know all the questions. Believe me, they will soon cease to matter much to you. This is the realm of first causes. Second causes fade into insignificance here."

"And Cain's wife?"

"Persistent too!" he laughed again. "That's good. You want truth to make sense. Let me just say that our concern here is not primarily with the sorts of questions that consume minds on the other side. We care that people learn to look inside themselves, and become all the Father created them to be. That is the deepest truth. It is the only truth. But your questions will eventually all be answered. Once the eternal truth of *becoming* is understood, most other questions cease to have much meaning. All truth is swallowed up in becoming."

"*Becoming*? Will I keep growing now that I am here? I thought that everyone would be…"

My voice faltered. I realized the presumption in the word that had been about to fall from my lips.

"*Perfect*, you mean?" he said.

"I confess…yes, that is what I was thinking," I replied.

"By no means," he answered. "Sinless, yes. Perfect no."

"I don't think I understand."

"One of the questions you were wondering about

29

earlier was how many of your ideas would turn out to be right, and which ones would be wrong."

I nodded.

"I am sorry to begin on a negative note, but since you brought it up—this is one of those prevalent notions that is grievously incorrect—that perfection is bestowed on believers instantly and automatically. Nothing could be further from the truth."

"And sin?" I asked.

"The sin nature drops away, and a great relief you will find that indeed. But there remains much growing to be done. As I said, a journey of discovery awaits you—full of joy, wonder, yes and even questions. It is a journey upward into the Logos Truth of heaven."

"I thought *you* were the Logos."

"I am an expression of the Logos, which is just the reality of the Father's universe. I pointed toward that Truth. Now you must continue to grow into it."

"I thought spiritual growth was for the purpose of getting into heaven."

"I am well acquainted with that fallacy as well," he said. There was no humor in his tone. Rather, almost a hint of frustration. "*Getting into heaven*, as you put it, is indeed one of the great misplaced priorities of Christendom. It goes hand in hand with that idol so falsely worshipped by many, *spiritual knowledge.* But neither knowledge nor getting into heaven are much prized here as indicators of spiritual maturity. They often reveal just the opposite. Getting into heaven, in and of itself, means far less than is supposed. You would be amazed how many arrive here utterly unfit for what lies ahead."

"Is that the case with me?" I asked a little timidly.

"I said that you had lived well. You prepared yourself for heaven by your life on earth. You are far advanced on the road to your becoming."

"What does matter most, then," I asked, "if not heaven?"

"Fulfilling the Father's purpose. You children are so concerned with the *where* that you lose sight of the *why*. Everyone must become what the Father envisioned them to be when he created them. Just like the roses you were so fond of, all must become the Father's flowers. Now that that you are here, the eternal process of becoming assumes new forms. You will move on from where your earthly life left off."

My questions were silenced for a time.

He glanced toward me. I thought I detected a twinkle returning to his eye. A hint of fun played on his lips. "As for Cain's wife," he added, "you will doubtless meet her one day. If it still matters at that time, you can ask her yourself where she came from. The answer may surprise you!"

SEVEN

The Angels' New Song

We turned a corner along one of the garden paths bordered by hedges on each side. Ahead a mound of earth, decorated with rocks and miniature plants and boulders, rose in front of the path.

I laughed with delight at the sight. It was the fulfilled vision of what we had built in the small space behind our own house, though three or four times larger!

The Lord saw my reaction and seemed pleased.

"I hoped you would like it!" he said.

The heavenly version of the waterfall and stream was not huge, perhaps six or eight feet in height, though larger than the one I had made with my own hands. Down three sides flowed several narrow streams. The water tumbled over rocks on all sides, flowed around a multitude of small trees and ferns and mosses and over several waterfalls before it rushed frothing and lyrical into a stone-lined pond some six feet across.

As I took in the sight, I wondered briefly if I were simply dreaming, or if I was somehow poised between life and death. The intense reality of my surroundings, however, soon dispelled such notions.

Beside the pond—certainly not like anything in our yard and garden!—sat a wide flat bench, ancient beyond years. It was a simple slab of stone, without back, pitted and worn, half covered with lichen. Faint writing seemed at one time to have been carved into the horizontal slab. It was so worn away by the years as to be unintelligible.

A harp stood in front of it. The bench was empty, but the strings were vibrating vigorously. The harp seemed to be playing itself, or was being played by invisible soft breezes. The notes from its strings filled the garden in perfect harmony with the splashing noises of the streams and waterfalls. The liquidy symphony resonated exquisitely to the harmonies of the harp.

We walked forward and stood in front of the stone bench.

Drinking in the music, I glanced to my side. A change was visible on the Lord's countenance. He seemed quietly, peacefully happy. His eyes were moist.

"This music always brings tears to my eyes," he said. "I gave her this song for exactly this purpose. My heart rejoices when another soul reaches home to these strains and joins those who have come before."

"I seem to recognize the melody," I said at length. "I'm sure I have heard it before, though without the watery accompaniment."

"You have indeed."

"Where did I hear it?"

"The harpist was playing it moments ago when you fell asleep. She is still playing it. This is her harp in your hospital room. No one has yet discovered that you are with me now."

"My wife doesn't know?"

"She is asleep. The music entered her soul just as it did yours. She was asleep within seconds."

"I saw that."

"She will be sad to know that she slept through your waking. But it is the Father's way. He often brings his sons and daughters home in the aloneness of earthly solitude."

"The music is extraordinary," I said. "I can't put my finger on it exactly. It has an aura of other-worldliness. The moment I heard it, I think that's when my journey here began."

"It is one of our oft-used transition themes. It helps many through the door enveloped in the peace of its mystical sounds."

"What is it called?" I asked.

He smiled. "The best way to answer you is to show you where I touched the strings that brought it to life."

"Did you give the lady the notes?"

"Nothing like that. We do not dictate specific outcomes from here."

"*We?*"

"My Father and our Spirit, and myself of course. Though we are one, all three of us work in distinct ways. We merely create influences through which individual personalities weave their unique talents and gifts and yieldings to our heavenly influences. It was entirely *her* song. But the strings of her heart were so in tune with my fingers on the strings of her harp, that the music coming from it that day was heard on both sides of eternity. Heads paused and many ears here turned toward the faint sounds as the song materialized. We realized that they resonated with eternal themes. Whenever it is heard now, the angels' ears perk up and they soon begin to sing. They know that another of

God's sons or daughters may soon be on their way home."

"I *thought* I heard angels singing!" I said, glancing about eagerly. "Where are they?"

"You will see them when it is time. But let us be going. You asked about the song. I will show you where it came into being."

To my astonishment, we walked straight through both harp and the solid stone of the bench as if they were not there. We continued into the mountain of streams and waterfalls and moved effortlessly through them as well.

"That was weird!" I exclaimed. "Was all that just a mirage—the harp and bench and rocks and waterfalls and streams?"

He laughed. "They were more real than anything you knew on earth—as solid as can be. Go back and touch them if you like."

"I will take your word for it," I replied. "How were we able to go through them?"

"Surely you are familiar with my walking through the wall into the room where my disciples were gathered after my own death as it was called?"

I nodded.

"Even though the wall was nothing to me, they were able to touch me and feel my hands and feet and body. I was not less real, I had become *more* real."

"I suppose they were just as surprised as I was."

"They were," the Lord chuckled fondly. "They had the added disadvantage of still being in the flesh when confronted by the reality of my eternal body. Those were challenging times for them. But their hearts were true, so they understood in time."

"I hope I will."

"You already are. The light brings much into focus. You too are now *more* real than the harp or the bench back there. Personhood is the most real thing in the universe. Now that your personhood has been transformed by the reality of eternity, your realness transcends mere mass. All realities change here."

"I am definitely discovering that!"

"But the essence of reality doesn't change, only its outer appearance. The smells and sounds and the very essence of these realities—especially the music—transcend the barriers between earth and heaven. When someone says that a melody or fragrance is ethereal or heavenly, they do not realize how true are those words."

I nodded as I took in his words.

"In your former world, mass and physicality were considered the true realities. Everything is now different. Mass and physicality continue to exist. But here they are *lesser* realities—ghostly, ephemeral, transitory—alongside the true realities of heaven."

"Which are?"

"The Father's will. The personhood of becoming. The unity of all things. And the Love that is the Life of heaven. You have entered into that Life. You have been imbued with the greater reality of eternity."

EIGHT

The Kirkyard

As the Lord spoke, our surroundings changed. The music of the streams and waterfalls modulated by degrees into the rustling of leaves in a wood of tall birch, beech, oak, and maple trees. We were walking in the midst of their shadows.

A tall stone wall rose in front of us. We continued on and walked straight through it. I found myself standing amid a random conglomeration of gravestones and markers, large and small, some straight, others leaning, most of ancient date. Among them here and there were scattered a number of wide flat slabs elevated a foot or two off the ground by thick vertical wedges of stone at each end. They apparently marked graves of important individuals. Most of the engravings were so worn by time that for all practical purposes the cemetery's most striking feature was anonymity.

In the center of the small cemetery rose a plain but beautiful old stone church. Windows of stained glass accented each end of four wings laid out in the shape of a cross. A pointed steeple rose high into the vault of blue above. Surrounding the church and cemetery extended the irregular stone wall through which we had just passed. Behind it towered the encircling grove of musical trees.

Near the church the same harp again stood in front of what earlier I had taken for a stone bench. I saw now that it was one of the flat grave markers.

On the slab memorializing the life of some departed saint of old, her fingers motionless on the strings of her harp, sat the lady from the hospital room. I recognized her instantly. She seemed waiting.

"Can she…" I whispered.

"No," smiled the Lord. "She thinks herself quite alone. She cannot hear us or see us. You may speak freely."

I watched for a moment. Except for the lyrical breezes above us, the churchyard was silent. The overtones in the trees were waiting for the harp to join in.

"Is this happening now?" I asked.

"All time here is *now*. She is years away from the day she will meet you and your wife in the hospital. But I must prepare her for that day."

"It seems I faintly hear her music among the breezes of the trees."

"You have a fine ear! But she does not hear it yet. She is making herself ready to hear it. Her spirit is listening. She has quieted herself into the Center where true hearing takes place."

He paused a moment, watching her with eyes of love.

"She is ready," he said at length.

He left me and walked toward her. He stood a moment facing her, a tender smile on his face. He reached out with both hands, set them on the strings, held them a few seconds as if imbuing them with life. Then he sent his hands slowly up and down the strings. They made no sound. Yet their vibrations transmitted themselves to the woman's hands. Almost immediately her fingers began to move. Slowly they plucked at the strings, probing tentatively at first, then gradually gaining strength. At last I heard them, random notes and chords at first but hinting at a far off melody floating in the air above us.

The Lord returned to where I stood. His expression was one of happiness.

"I love this!" he said. "When a soul stills and allows itself to dwell, even for a few moments, in the quiet Center, wonderful things happen. She is beginning to hear the music."

"I am hearing it in the trees. How can she just now be making it up?"

"The music already exists within her. It is stirring in her depths. She *feels* it. She simply hasn't yet turned it into a song. First she must tune herself to the rhythms of her heart, which is what you hear in the breezes. Gradually the notes will reveal themselves to her fingers. I touched the strings to help her discover them."

Unconsciously I glanced around again at the gravestones surrounding us.

"Yes," the Lord nodded, reading my thoughts, "she is thinking of the saints whose unknown names are on these markers. She has entered into harmony with the themes of eternity. That is why the song that is beginning to flow will contain power in both realms."

"Where are we?" I asked glancing about. "I would guess this to be an ancient church in Scotland. I think I may recognize it."

"You and your wife visited here once. The song is called *Cullen Kirkyard*...or it will be when she completes it."

"And this is the song she played in my hospital room?"

He nodded with a smile. He was obviously aware of my perplexity over the fluidity of past and present.

We turned and walked out of the churchyard. We left through a great black iron gate—I'm not sure whether it was opened or closed, nor did it matter. As we went I heard the recognizable strains of the song drifting up from the harp over the cemetery behind us to join the accompanying breezes of beech and oak.

The gravestones and church and trees faded from sight. A moment later we were again standing beside the harp and bench in front of the waterfalls, streams, and pool. The bench in front of me was the grave-slab from the churchyard. It was empty now. The woman was gone. The strings of the harp in front of it were still. The music had stopped.

When the Lord spoke, his voice contained sadness.

"Your wife is now awake," he said. "The harpist I sent to play you through your waking is comforting her. Both of them know that you are with me now. Your wife is weeping. But her tears are not lost. The Father is collecting them in his heart. Every one will be given back as sparkling heavenly diamonds on the day she meets me here."

"May I see her?" I asked.

"It is best I comfort her alone."

He turned, again walked into the harp, and disappeared.

I stood in front of the pond listening to the pleasant streams and waterfalls. I was alone mere seconds. Again the Lord was beside me.

"Your wife is a dear lady," he said. "I held her in my arms a few moments. She will endure and grow strong through her pain, and grow to love you even more. The Spirit is with her of course, and will remain in her heart."

"If you don't mind my asking, what is happening now?"

"The room is filling with doctors and nurses. They saw the change on the monitors. This will be a difficult time for your wife. But she is in good hands. She and the harpist will meet again. They will form a lasting friendship. It is your wife's story now. As much as you would like to comfort her, that part of your life's saga is behind you. As she must temporarily let you go, so must you let her go. It is time for you to leave the garden and begin your journey."

"My journey...where?"

"To the High Places. To the Mountains. To my Father's Realm."

"I would love to hear the harpist play again," I said as we walked away and the water faded behind us. "Especially now that I know the genesis of the music."

"You will."

"When?"

"At your funeral."

"Oh...yes, of course. I didn't think of that. Will she play *Cullen Kirkyard?*"

"Probably not. Your wife yet has little idea of the role played by the final song emanating from the harp in bringing you to me, nor that it has become one of the melodies favored by the angels. The music of the spheres, which is just the music of heaven, is often too subtle for earthly ears to recognize. More likely your wife will choose some of your favorite hymns for the occasion."

"I will enjoy that too. Imagine—saying that I am looking forward to my own funeral!" I added with a laugh.

"It is good to hear you laugh," rejoined the Lord. "That is another adjustment people often have to make after their arrival—the realization that humor is alive and well in heaven. Some of the more pious types find it not somber enough for their tastes. But in truth there is a great deal of laughter here."

NINE

Reunions

I was still thinking about what the Lord had said.

"Is not all heaven the Father's Realm?" I asked.

"Certainly," he replied. "But remember what I told my disciples—in my Father's house are *many* rooms. This garden is but your doorway. There are many doorways through which the faithful enter, as well as many mansions. They all have much to contribute to your becoming."

We left the garden—my doorway into heaven, as he had called it—in the direction of the open meadows and fields and woodlands. Soon, however, its paths disappeared and I felt cement beneath my feet. We were again in the city, surrounded on all sides by buildings and traffic and bustle.

Ahead we neared a large modern building surrounded by a huge parking lot. I recognized it instantly. It seemed like only yesterday I was there with my wife walking toward the church on the day after our anniversary.

"It's my church!" I exclaimed.

The Lord smiled. "There are a few people who have been waiting to see you," he said.

At his words the doors flew open and a great crowd poured out.

"It must be noon," I said. "The service has just concluded."

"Not exactly," he rejoined with a humorous smile. "Some of these people have been waiting for you for centuries."

"Where was there possibly room for them all?" I exclaimed, laughing at the sight. "The church isn't that big!"

The throng grew into a multitude. They were not coming just from the church, but from all around— from the city, from the countryside beyond. A host of what appeared thousands streamed toward me. They were pouring out of the surrounding hills, coming from everywhere!

At my side, the Lord was still smiling. When a moment later I glanced in his direction again, he had disappeared.

I saw my parents leading the way from the church, running toward me with huge smiles on their faces.

My father's health had never been the best. He had been virtually crippled by the time he was fifty. Here he was a vigorous man of thirty or forty sprinting over the ground with giant strides.

Beside him and keeping pace, my mother was radiant and beautiful. I had never seen such a gorgeous woman!

My dear mother! And my strong, manly, noble father!

My heart filled with indescribable emotion. This was the man and woman whose love for one another had given me life.

They *loved* me! What a liberating, joyous, heart-expanding truth. *Love* had birthed me into being!

I wept as they came. Warm tears of happiness flowed like rivers down my cheeks. I heard my voice laughing at the sight, giggling like a boy. I was a child again!

In the merest instant, the remembrance swept through me of what the Lord said about the different realities of heaven. Was I now seeing the *personhood* of my father and mother for the first time, rather than their physical bodies? Were these the people they had *become*, and were *becoming*? Did I now know them because I was seeing *into* them? What I recognized was the real man and the real woman, the *eternal* man and woman.

I had no time to speculate further. The physical reality of the reunion was equally real. Suddenly we were hugging and kissing, my father slapping me on the shoulder and my mother kissing my face and all three of us talking at once.

"We have been watching for you for days!" said my mother. "Well...days, in *your* time. I couldn't wait to see you!"

"She's been impossible!" laughed my father. "She's been gazing off in the distance in every direction. Every few minutes she would exclaim, *Here he comes...I think I see him!* Suddenly I would see her pointing somewhere else. *There he is—look, look...over there!*"

"I haven't been able to sleep a wink," laughed my mother.

"Do you sleep here?" I asked in surprise.

She had to think a minute. "I don't know what to call it," she said. "It's something like it in a way, but much better than sleep."

"Once word began to circulate that you were coming," said my father, "the crowd began to gather in and around the church. As you can see, there were a lot of people who wanted to be here."

"They let us greet you first," said my mother. "That is always the custom."

"Who are they all!" I laughed, glancing at the horde behind them.

"Your relatives and ancestors," answered my father. "You will know them all soon enough. And here are two I have been waiting years for you to meet," he added eagerly.

He turned and opened one arm to greet another man and woman hurrying up behind him. To all appearance they were the same age, equally strong and radiant, and likewise beaming with wide smiles on their faces.

"These are my parents," said my father. "Your grandfather and grandmother."

Again I was assaulted by hugs and kisses and exuberant words of welcome.

"From Oklahoma!" I exclaimed. "This is fantastic. All my life I wanted to meet you!"

"Now you have the rest of eternity to know us," said my grandfather. "Do you play checkers?"

"I have," I laughed. "Though I wouldn't call myself an aficionado. Why?"

"I became rather fond of the game during the Depression—nothing else to do, you know. My affection for it never left me, not even here. Who would have thought it," he added, laughing, "—checkers in heaven. One of the first things I learned was that earthly loves don't disappear. It's actually quite a fun place once you get used to it. Why everyone wouldn't want to spend eternity in heaven is beyond me. Anyway, on the subject of checkers, quite a few of us get together to play."

"I will look forward to it."

"I must warn you—it is a little more complicated here. We play the game in three dimensions…and the real masters play in four."

"That must be something to see!"

"Games go on for years."

"I'm also looking forward to meeting my cousins on your side of the family. There must have been—"

"Five hundred thirty seven if you go out to seconds and thirds," said my grandmother proudly. "We had twenty nine grandchildren. Most of them and their extended families have come to see you."

"Say, did they ever catch the fellow who shot you?" asked my father where he stood beside his father.

"I don't know, Dad. It's only been a few days. It hardly seems to matter now."

"I realize that. But you know me—I always loved a good mystery. I've been trying to follow the police reports, but one is kept so busy here."

I laughed. "Ever the sleuth!" I said. "Perry Mason and Columbo! My last memory of you—back then, I mean—was with an Agatha Christie in your hand."

Even as I was visiting with my father and his parents, I glanced about at the throng descending upon us.

I saw my two other grandparents, my mother's parents, now coming up to join us. I had known them as a boy. I recognized them immediately.

"Grandma…Grandpa!" I exclaimed. "You are so young! You look just like the picture in our bedroom. What a delight to see you!"

"We want you to meet our son Daryl," said my grandmother. "He died as an infant, you remember.

Neither you nor your mother had the chance to know him."

My eyes took in the man standing beside her, the son of her womb whom she had known but for a few brief hours in their previous life. He was now a fully mature man of heaven. The expression on his countenance was remarkably unlike that of anyone around him—quiet and full of peace. My first thought was that he must be an angel. Then the realization filled me that he was a heavenly being almost between the angels and those of glorified humanity. He was a sinless human being. His becoming had taken place, not within the confines and weaknesses of the fleshly nature, but within the Father's heart. He was of that special number specially chosen by God to be snatched out of the world early, and thus to arrive in heaven unstained by sin. He had arrived in heaven fully flowering as a perfect blossom of the Father's thought.

"Uncle Daryl," I said, awed by the sight of my mother's brother, "it is an honor to meet you."

Within seconds I was swallowed in the surging human tide behind them. Singing and rejoicing, smiles and laughter, hugs and kisses, all engulfed me. The happy reunions and introductions went on for hours.

I met my eight great grandparents, and sixteen great-great grandparents, and great-greats farther back than I could count.

Every one had contributed to the man I was. I was hungry to know everything. I wanted to spend a year with each one! Somehow I knew that this was only the beginning, and that I *would* be able to spend a year with anyone I wanted to...or a thousand years...eons...playing checkers or discussing Agatha Christie with my father, or delving into deep spiritual topics.

There were aunts and uncles, and great aunts and uncles going back too many generations to count, cousins innumerable and of such complexity of connection it would be impossible to remember.

I met many of my Borton, Packer, and Woolman ancestors who had come to America in the 17th century, others who had fought in the Revolutionary and Civil wars...on both sides of both wars...and in the English Civil war, and on both sides of that one too. Our whole family tree that my sister and I had worked so hard on through the years suddenly came to life.

The surprise reunions were infinitely varied. Hearing of the earthly lives of the myriad ancestors who met me was like a gigantic history lesson and family reunion rolled into one.

Earthly history, that is. More important were the stories of spiritual history. The history of individual "becoming" was the only true history that mattered to any of them.

No one was especially eager to tell me about the earthly times when they had lived. They wanted to share what they had learned and how they had grown since arriving in heaven. They wanted to recount every conversation they had had and tell me about the interesting guides that had been sent to instruct and mentor them along in their journeys.

I think the most distant relative I met was a seventeenth cousin, forty-two times removed if I have it straight. She said she had lived in the Middle Ages when times on earth were unbelievably difficult. It was not hard to see the becoming that had taken place in *her* heart! Her countenance was radiant.

How long the reunion went on, I have no idea. It must have been hours. Perhaps it was even weeks. Actually, it must have been years!

Gradually the crowd began to disperse. At length I was left with my father and mother.

"We will see you again, son," said my father. "Often in fact."

"How will I know where to find you, Dad?" I asked.

My father laughed with delight. "Believe me, you will know!" he said. "We *all* know where to find one another. Besides, you will be living close to us."

"*Living?*" I said. "What do you mean—in a *house*...living where?"

"I forgot. I shouldn't have said anything. We call them mansions here. They are not houses exactly...but never mind all that. Everything will be explained."

TEN

Two Worlds Merge

My father and mother walked off hand in hand, slowly disappearing as into a mist. Again the Lord was with me.

"Did you enjoy that?" he asked.

"Immensely!" I answered enthusiastically. "It was amazing! And my parents! Have you seen—"

The smile on the Lord's face stopped me.

I laughed at how ludicrous was the question I had been about to ask.

"Yes," he said. "I know them quite well. I am very fond of your father."

My heart warmed at his words.

"And I have been doing my best to teach your grandfather the intricacies of four-dimensional checkers. But we have thousands of years. He will eventually master it."

Quietness descended between us.

"I want to answer the prayer you prayed on the morning after your anniversary," the Lord went on, "— the morning of your transition."

"What prayer was that?" I said. "I've already forgotten."

"You were wondering what heaven is like."

"Oh, right—of course."

"You have already discovered some of the answers. Now it is time for you to learn to see people as I see them. Come with me."

He turned and I followed.

We left the precincts of the church. I found myself walking along a busy street in the same city where my wife and I lived—or, where I *had* lived.

As I walked beside the Lord, I was conscious of a stillness, as if I were being carried along in a bubble of translucence, detached from the world's commotion on every side. Simultaneously I found that we were drawing near a crowded supermarket at midday. Cars sped by, engines were revving, radios blasting, horns blaring, people coming and going. The din of the city jarred my senses. What an incongruity to be with *him* in a place like this rather than on a peaceful Galilean hillside of some bygone era. The whole scene was vaguely familiar, as if this was the market where my wife and I shopped.

The brightness surrounding us faded. Had we traversed through an invisible door between the worlds? Much was happening that I did not fully grasp.

Wondering what we were doing here, the Lord replied to my question before I could ask it.

"I brought you here in answer to your prayer," he said. "We always answer the prayer the heart intends. We don't pay much attention to words. The Father and Spirit and I listen to hearts, not tongues. To answer your heart, therefore…heaven was everywhere, around you and within you."

I was still somewhat perplexed as I looked around at my surroundings.

"You must learn to see with the vision of heaven before you can perceive its wonders," he went on. "You have already learned to see a great deal. Now you will see more. It was among those you encountered every day, all your life, that you learned to see with heaven's eyes."

"Was I learning that?" I asked.

"You set yourself to learn my ways years ago. Your heart's desire was to live an upright compassionate life. That desire enabled you to begin the transformation of seeing with heaven's eyes. You spent your life learning to *see*, as we mean the word here—to see God's men and women, and all God's creatures, as we see them."

With the words, he vanished from sight.

I was near the entrance of the supermarket. A small girl was sitting on the curb of the sidewalk beside a box upon which were printed the words *Free Kittens*. Her face was smudged, her hair matted. Her dirty dress amounted to no more than a cloak of rags. She might well have stepped off the pages of a Dickens novel. I smiled down at her, wondering if she could see me, then walked into the busy store.

All about was commotion, activity, and noise. A sight more at odds with the peace of heaven I could scarcely imagine. The men and women around me were rushed, stressed, and agitated, caught up, almost as animals in a trap, in the urgent pace of modern society—unseeing of one another, unperceiving that they were God's precious children.

My heart smote me with love for my kind. Tears rose in my eyes, and I knew them for real tears this time. Was I feeling what the Lord himself had felt when gazing upon Jerusalem and lamenting for his people?

My attention was diverted as an argument broke out at one of the check stands over a disputed charge.

Nearby a harried mother desperately tried to keep a difficult toddler from toppling a display of cookies.

Down another aisle an irritated father yelled at a wild five year old.

In several of the other check out lines, disgruntled shoppers muttered frustrations while inefficient clerks took three times longer than necessary with each customer.

The very air of the store was suffocating in the stressful energy of anxiety, impatience, edginess, irritation, and unpeace.

I stood staring at each face. Time slowed. I saw *into* every one on whom my eyes rested. The hubbub of noise and commotion receded into silence.

It was the way of heaven. I was able to enter invisibly into earth's life. But none on the other side were aware that heaven was in, through, and all around them—permeating, interpenetrating, and saturating their lives. How could they know that earth and heaven were not separate at all, but occupied the same universe, the same space, the same life?

I walked about as if I had entered into the heart of a moment. I could move and think. Yet about me no time went by. I was *between* time. I beheld the faces anew. I should say that their faces were revealed to me with new eyes of seeing.

Was this what the Lord meant with his use of the word *Behold*?

As I moved invisibly among them, the people in the crowded market slowly changed before my eyes. Out of the hurry and frustration, I saw emerge here and there radiant expressions of childlikeness.

An elderly woman, full of wrinkles, back stooped and humped, hair of pure white, gradually stood up tall, erect, and strong. Her hump disappeared. She was transformed before my eyes into a spectacular and beautiful young woman of thirty—her face calm, serene, quietly joyful and full of love. Somehow, I could not exactly tell why, she reminded me of the girl with the kittens…almost—strange thought—as if I were seeing the same person at different stages of life.

Not all the changes were pleasant to behold.

As I watched the woman with wonder, a man came up behind her. He was perhaps thirty-five or forty years of age, his acidic face twisted with aggravation and annoyance.

"Get out of my way, you old fool!" he barked, crowding past her. "You're taking up the whole aisle. There *are* other people trying to get around the store, you know!"

The crippled woman, ancient to his unseeing eyes, glanced up and returned his caustic words with a kindly smile.

As I stared at him, the man's face grew hard and cold. Years suddenly passed before my eyes like seconds. Age consumed him. Bitterness deepened in his eyes. Wrinkles of anger crowded one upon the other. His skin whitened, splotched with brown cancerous spots, stretched thinly over a gaunt and bony frame.

Within seconds he stood in front of me stooped and feeble, decrepit and ugly, a scowl of animosity on his face. A foul and offensive odor poured out of him. It was the putrid smell of death.

I turned away in disgust.

ELEVEN

Spirit Vision

All about such transformations were taking place. Slowly I made my way through the store, sickened and marveling at once. Some individuals were metamorphisizing into nothing less than angels. Others became grotesque and hideous demons. Small children turned into radiant beings of peace. Others were transformed into aged, pitiful malodorous creatures that revolted my senses.

In their midst I beheld an ethereal, semi-transparent figure of white. He—or she...I could not tell—was gliding silently and invisibly among them, speaking yet without sound. The robed phantasm—*apparently* robed in white, though again, I could not tell—was speaking into regions within each one where listening did not proceed from the ears, but from deeper realms of consciousness.

At first I thought I was seeing a ghost. And in truth, I was not far wrong.

Some turned toward the unseen Voice, seeing nothing but sensing impulses toward right, toward goodness, toward kindness. Others, however, were heedless of the unheard urgings of the heavenly Specter. They went about their business unmoved and unchanged by the strange encounter.

Even as my eyes followed the figure, I knew that he—or she—was likewise speaking to *me*...deeper than thought, deeper than emotion, deeper even than conscience...confirming, testing, illuminating, goading, guiding, convicting, calming, reassuring, and *quickening* Life within me.

It was the Voice of the Spirit revealing the Father and Son into the lives of humanity in a myriad of individual ways.

I knew that the same Spirit had been within me, speaking and illuminating truth throughout my life, pricking my conscience toward right, goading and impelling me, as all men and all women and all children, toward righteousness, and toward the divine Fatherhood.

For a moment the translucent Specter vanished. A few seconds later I saw it reappear, emerging from out of a lonely woman walking the aisles with a look of desperation on her face. I knew that the Spirit was not merely speaking *to* her but had entered deep *inside* her to comfort and heal her aching heart.

It now came toward me. I knew it was gazing into me. But the whiteness was too bright to see its face. Warmth emanated from its approach—the warmth of comfort, reassurance, and peace.

The white Ghost of heaven entered into me and filled me and inundated me with pure light. And I was swept inside its Life even as it filled my own. I felt the presence of Father and Son, each speaking in a language beyond words their individual revelations into my soul.

God above. God beside. God within. The three were one, as I was one with them.

And the Lord's words reverberated in my being:

May they be one as we are one, as you, Father, are in me and I am in you, that they may also be in us—I in them and you in me, that they may be perfectly one.

And I was swept away in a rapture of joy to be one with my Maker. I knew I was praying, though in no audible tongue of man, but in the silent language of heaven in which they were likewise speaking into me.

The next instant I perceived the silent Spirit of Indwellingness move through me and to others in need. Yet it had not left me, and would never leave me.

Whether I was in the market five seconds or five years, I could not say. Gradually life around me resumed its pace. I left the store.

The girl still sat on the sidewalk with her box of kittens. If anything, her dress was dirtier and even more threadbare. She was in every way a street urchin. I was almost afraid to look. What might *she* become before my eyes?

Yet I was comforted with the thought, for behind her shone a great light, and I knew the Spirit was at work.

I perceived that the girl could see me. She glanced up and smiled. I stooped beside her and returned her smile. My heart filled again with love for her childlike innocence.

"Why are you giving away your kittens?" I asked as I gazed into her eyes.

"Because there are too many," she replied. "My mommy says we can't keep them. I am trying to find them a new home."

She peered with longing into my face. Her eyes were so full of liquid light it seemed they would swallow mine into them.

"Would you like one, sir?" she asked sweetly. "They are good kittens."

My heart melted.

"Yes," I smiled. "I will take one of your kittens."

"Oh, thank you!" she exclaimed. She pushed the box toward me. "You may pick one yourself."

I reached in and gently took hold of a small white ball of fur. She thanked me again. I stood to go.

Already the girl was changing. The figure of white came forward, entered into the girl, and disappeared from my vision.

The girl stood and grew tall. Behind her, I saw two new images of white. These I knew to be angels standing on either side of her. The two heavenly guardians were staring at her with eyes of worshipful adoration. The face between them lengthened and aged and brightened. The two eyes filled with yet more light, until—another chill swept through me!—suddenly the angels were gone and the Lord stood again before me!

At the same instant a strange fluttering drew my eyes. The tiny kitten was squirming about in my hands. I loosened my grip. I beheld that I was no longer holding a kitten. Some winged creature was coming to life. My own hands had become the chrysalis of its transformation.

I opened my palms and held them aloft. With a flurry of feathers and wings it fluttered out of my hand and soared aloft. Its wingspan quickly grew. As it ascended into the sky, I followed its motion until I was gazing upon a giant dove of purest white, its feathers tinged with radiance as of from the sun itself. It disappeared into the deep blue of the heavens.

I returned my eyes to the earth. The Lord knew what was the unspoken question on my lips.

"The winged prayer-dove has taken your vision of heaven," he said, "and your kindness to the girl, back to their home in the Father's heart."

TWELVE

Heaven in Earth's Midst

Our steps took us away from the supermarket. The turmoil and tumult of the city faded. We were soon walking up a gently sloping hillside in the middle of the country. Trees grew at wide intervals. Under our feet spread a thin carpet of grass. My heart was quiet.

"Do you understand what the Spirit has revealed to you?" asked the Lord.

"That the people I used to encounter in life were not what they seem?" I said.

"In part," he answered. "In another way they *are* what they seem, if you have eyes to see what the Spirit reveals. Now that you are here, you no longer see with earthly eyes. Deep vision into the heart of things is one of the most important changes that comes with waking. You have made it, because you are making it."

I pondered the complexity of his words.

"My Father and I see what people are becoming," he continued, "what they are making themselves. Such vision you now possess. That elderly woman in the market only looked stooped and bowed to earthly sight.

To my eyes, for much of her life she has been a radiant daughter of heaven. What you beheld as she was transformed was no mere vision. It was the reality of becoming. *She* did not change. Your vision changed. Such she truly *is*. It is her present earthly body that is fleeting and transitory."

"What about her," I said, "the old woman—is she…is she *here* now—in heaven? Have I been looking into her past?"

"Past and present are all one here. There is no past. All is *now*. On another plane, however, she is still dwelling in her earthly frame. To those nearby she appears much as you first saw her. You were given a vision of what she will look like when you next meet her. You will recognize her instantly, not for her earthly features but for what you will behold in her eyes."

"When will I see her?" I asked eagerly.

"At the appointed time."

"And the man?" I asked.

The Lord's eyes filled with sorrow. "He is greatly admired by his peers," he replied, "—a success in his field, handsome and wealthy. He has turned many women's hearts and made a great deal of money. Men envy his supposed success and status. Neither he nor his admirers have any inclination what he is turning himself into, and thus what he actually is. You saw the character he is forming within himself."

"Why don't you warn him?" I asked.

"The Spirit is constantly doing so," he replied. "You beheld the Spirit among them. Yet the self-satisfied rarely heed the inner Voice. They do not understand the imperative of spiritual hunger. They are unseeing of the revelations about them. Dozens of revelations come to that man daily. They come in the children and women he passes and the men with whom he has dealings. They are about him in the fragrance of the sweet pea, in the kiss of the breeze on his cheeks, in the myriad smiles sent his way, in the warmth of the sun on his skin, in the glories of the sunset, in the countless kindnesses shown him that he does not notice. The Spirit's presence surrounds him everywhere! He has encountered angels more times than even I am aware of. But he is unseeing, unhearing, unperceiving. The Spirit's Voice is *always* speaking. But his ears are dull. He is living for himself. He is unable to hear, for he has not set himself to *become* a man whose life will please the Father."

We walked for some time in silence.

"And what of me?" I asked. "What am I becoming? What do your eyes see when you look at *me*?"

He smiled.

"One who used his life to mature and develop his personhood."

"And *how* is personhood developed?" I asked.

"By one's choices. It is how all spiritual muscle is developed. Do you see that woman walking toward us?"

I looked ahead and saw a woman of middle age approaching. She took no notice of us.

"Yes, but I don't recognize her," I said.

"You scarcely knew her. Your lives crossed paths but for a moment. Yet a simple smile from you changed her life and set her on her own path of becoming."

"I don't remember."

"There was a day you were in a government office waiting your turn. All around were men and women frustrated, tense, and anxious. You took notice of a crippled woman who appeared troubled. Your heart went out to her. Some time later, she approached and asked you for the time. You smiled broadly and tried to make your smile penetrate her heart as you gave her the time. She had had a very difficult day. Your kind words gave her a boost she badly needed. Your smile *did* penetrate. The Spirit was there insuring that your kindness went where it was supposed to go inside her. That small moment set the dear woman on course to begin believing in herself. She is here now. You will meet her later. She will express her gratitude personally."

I listened in humble awe to realize how filled with import were the small moments of life.

"There were countless lives your kindness touched," the Lord went on. "So it is with all those who dedicate themselves to obedience. And *you* were changed by every act of kindness too—changed into a person a little more like me. That's the person you were turning yourself into."

The Lord paused and smiled.

"In other words," he said, "to answer your question—as I told you when we met, I see a man who lived well, who set himself to become God's child. And now I have shown you these things to prepare you for your continued growth. I have revealed to you how thoroughly the worlds of heaven and earth are intertwined. As you will discover, however, most of the visitations to the earthly realm in which you will participate will take place beyond the ken of earthly perceptions. You will come and go as do the angels, though their mandate is of course quite different. But for both you and the angels, the worlds thoroughly interpenetrate. Only those with the Father's eyes are able to perceive it."

"And the little girl?" I asked at length.

"She is but another form in which I visit the world of men in order that they might learn to see with the Spirit's eyes. Take my words into your heart and you will understand all, *Whatever you have done or said to one of the least of these, you have done and said to me.*"

THIRTEEN

Personal Visitations

A gain our surroundings changed.
       Soon we were making our way through the
streets and along the sidewalks of a small rural town.
We walked into a café bustling with breakfast
customers. Here, too, the white ghostly image of the
Spirit was moving among and into and out of the men
and women of the place. I was mesmerized as I gazed
into faces, listened to conversations, and heard and saw
with the perceptions of heaven. My vision of some of
the faces rejoiced my heart, others brought tears to my
eyes. If only I could speak to them! If only I could
make them see and hear the truth of becoming!

We moved on to a hardware store…then the police
department… through the jail…then into a crowded
courtroom filled with television cameras. Everywhere
the Spirit was present…speaking, convicting,
instructing, illuminating, comforting.

In the courtroom a trial was in progress. As I
looked about, I was surprised to see my wife and sons
and our pastor and many friends whom I recognized in
the courtroom. They were all noticeably older than

when I last saw them, though that was seemingly such a short time before.

I glanced at the Lord with question.

"It is the trial of the man convicted of your murder," he said. "He is about to be sentenced to execution."

At the word I could not help thinking of the Lord's own trial and crucifixion. Instead of my wife, my eyes were inexplicably drawn to the man, head down, who sat silently awaiting his fate. The Spirit hovered about him a long time. I wondered if any part of his consciousness was aware of its presence.

Though I could not see his face clearly, my heart went out to the man. I recalled the Lord's tender words to the thief condemned at his side, "Today you will be with me in paradise."

I looked again to my side. The Lord was weeping.

I heard and saw nothing more of the proceedings. As quickly as the other changes had come upon us, I found myself in the halls of a high school at lunch hour. The place was teeming with young people. Around me were incomplete protoplasmic souls progressing toward their eternal futures as men and women of character, grace, integrity, and kindness. Others revealed themselves unhappy, selfish, bitter loners in the making.

No one saw me. I was among them, seeing into them, observing their becoming. But they knew nothing of my presence.

Again came a change. We were walking through a crowded city mall...then a bank...across the lawn of a university campus...then through the aisles of Congress, all with the same result.

We entered a high rise and took the elevator to one of the top floors. We walked into the headquarters of a major computer and marketing firm. All around were faces and eyes and conversations of *becoming*. But the men and women of corporate ambition were unaware that heaven was in their midst. Some were becoming *higher* beings, most were becoming something *lower*. Every human soul was in process toward becoming or decay.

We spent much time walking the corridors of a large hospital. Suffering lay close on every side. To my right and left I perceived God's angels of light throughout the hospital sent to give comfort and peace. The Lord went into every room and laid his hand gently on the suffering and dying. Wherever he went, the angels retreated reverently to allow him to minister personally.

As we made our way along a long corridor, I sensed our surroundings changing. They were no longer so modern. Earth time seemed tumbling back, decade upon decade.

We approached two double doors. Above them a sign read, "Maternity Ward."

We continued inside. A doctor was supervising a birth. Several nurses were assisting him. A man stood across the room observing with obvious anxiety.

It was my father!

And lying on the table, perspiring and in the pain of labor, was my *mother*!

I watched in awe. I knew that I was beholding my own birth into the world of men.

I glanced at the Lord. I could tell that my face was filled with the stunned expression of many emotions.

"I wanted you to see the great love that gave you life," he said. "Entering into the hearts of these two, your own parents, at this wonderful moment in their lives, will complete the life-circle of your own self-knowing."

I walked across the floor to my father. Unseen, I took my place at his side and watched with him. With indescribable emotion to be with him at such a time, I recalled my feelings as I witnessed the birth of my own sons. The realization that my father felt a similar paternal love for *me* was almost too overwhelming to take in. Yet I knew I must take in the great truth, as the Lord said, to complete my own becoming.

I had always wondered if my own sons would ever know how deep was my love for them. Now I realized that, in their own appointed time, they *would* know.

Moments later, the first infant cries of my father's and mother's newborn son echoed through the small hospital room.

I wept to see the joy on their faces.

FOURTEEN

Nativity Come to Life

L eaving the hospital, I heard two nurses in the lobby parting ways for the evening.

"What are you doing tomorrow for Christmas?" asked one.

"Actually, I'm working."

"That's too bad."

"I don't mind. I offered. Extra pay, you know. I've got no family nearby. If I can help make the day special for a few people who are stuck here, it will be a day well spent."

"That's nice of you."

"What about you? Big plans?"

"The usual—the kids, the grands, presents, big dinner, turkey and the fixings."

"Sounds fun. I'll see you in a couple days, then. Merry Christmas!"

"And to you...even if you do have to work."

So, I thought, it was Christmas Eve. What an interesting time to be a heavenly onlooker!

The Lord and I walked through the doors and out into the chilly air of a winter's evening.

On the expansive lawn in front of the hospital a life-size nativity scene was set up. A small ensemble of carolers, bundled brightly in thick layers against the cold, stood to one side singing *O Little Town of Bethlehem.* A few people paused to listen on their way in or out of the hospital. The turnout seemed sparse for Christmas Eve. I suppose people coming and going from a hospital had other things on their minds than nativity scenes and Christmas carols.

The words floating across the night air were astonishing given that I was standing beside the very Messiah whose nativity this was. I was carried away as I listened with nostalgic memories of Christmases past.

O morning stars together, proclaim the holy birth, and praises sing to God the King, and peace to men on earth.

I began singing along. With the scene in the Maternity Ward so fresh in my mind, the memories flooding my mind were full of my parents and the holidays of childhood.

O holy Child of Bethlehem, descend on us we pray...O come to us, abide with us, our Lord Emmanuel.

I glanced beside me. Perhaps like mine witnessing my parents in the birthing room, the Lord's face wore emotions difficult to characterize. What must he be thinking as he took in this simple observance of *his* birth, and to hear the words the beloved carol spoke about him?

After a few minutes, he led me away. We continued into the city.

Sights and sounds of Christmas were evident everywhere. Shoppers bustled about. Families walking together, bright lights, colorfully wrapped packages, music coming from stores and shops as we passed, all contributed to the festive atmosphere.

Yet here was the Lord himself among them...and no one saw him! Would they recognize him if he were to make himself visible and known?

In the bright lit town square, a church choir was singing. Their carols could be heard throughout most of the downtown. As the strains of *The First Noel* rose into the air, we crossed the street and moved toward the scene.

The first noel, the angel did say, was to certain poor shepherds in fields where they lay.

In fields where they lay keeping their sheep, on a cold winter's night that was so deep.

Noel, noel...Noel, noel, born is the King of Israel.

A few shoppers stood by listening and singing along. Most of the comers and goers, however, were too intent on their last-minute errands to heed the high significance of the music around them—the reality of the incarnation, that the God of the universe had become flesh and dwelt among them.

We walked away from the square. The touching prayer of *Away in a Manger*—so pregnant with eternal meaning—receded softly behind us.

Be near me, Lord Jesus, I ask Thee to stay
Close by me forever, and love me I pray.
Bless all the dear children in Thy tender care,
Prepare us for heaven, to live with Thee there.

Outside several stores, Salvation Army volunteers in Santa hats stood ringing their bells and greeting passers-by.

I paused at the store window of a department store displaying a crèche behind its large plate-glass window. Something about it drew my attention. Perhaps it was simply the *fact* of it—a representation of Jesus' birth, when his eternal Presence was standing beside me.

"Do you see that shimmery whiteness in the corner of the window?" he asked.

"I think so," I replied. "Faintly."

"An angel is standing there."

"Really!" I exclaimed. "All I see is a shadowy light."

"She is there. Angels are sent as heaven's praying presence wherever a manger scene goes up—in homes, stores, on front lawns, in churches and schools...large, small, every one. I visit them all too."

"I had no idea. I saw no angels at the hospital."

"If you had looked carefully, you would have seen bursts of light now and then. The angels are there...in great abundance, actually."

Walking through the main entrance of a downtown mall, I glanced at the Lord as we passed a line of children waiting to visit a Santa in the atrium near the Food Court.

"I don't mind the Santa tradition so much," he said as we took in the scene. "Though it does not penetrate much past the surface, it focuses children on the importance of goodness. That reminder is healthy. I would rather that the imperative of kindness were not associated with the obsession for expensive gifts. But there are worse things in the world. The meaning of my birth will come alive in their hearts in time. Then will Christmas be fulfilled indeed."

We moved out of the downtown, passing church after church, some dark and quiet, others with services in progress, many with nativities in front. I peered intently at each one, beginning gradually to detect occasional wisps of brightness among them.

We came to a great cathedral. Through its closed doors and thick walls, the sounds of a large choir resounded from inside.

Joy to the world, the Lord is come, let earth receive her King. Let every heart prepare Him room.

And heaven and nature sing, and heaven and nature sing, and heaven and heaven and nature sing.

"Are there angels here?" I asked. "In the church, I mean."

"Of course," he replied.

We listened to several more triumphant carols in exquisite four part harmony. The Lord seemed particularly to enjoy it. Gradually we walked on as the familiar melody of the great Christmas hymn echoed behind us.

Silent night, holy night. All is calm, all is bright.

Round yon virgin, mother and child.

Holy infant, so tender and mild.

Sleep in heavenly peace, sleep in heavenly peace.

We returned to the square in the middle of the city. More music met our ears as we approached.

Come and behold Him, born the King of angels...

Sing choirs of angels, sing in exultation...

Glory to God, all glory in the highest...

O come, let us adore him...Christ, the Lord.

We did not stop this time. We returned at length to the hospital.

We stood watching and listening outside. The small group of carolers seemed louder than before. By now I could definitely detect filmy bursts of whiteness among them, some hovering in the air round about.

Then came a remarkable change.

As I watched, slowly the scene of Bethlehem's miracle came to life! Donkeys and cows and a camel shuffled about. Mary and Joseph stood over the straw-filled manger. Their eyes, like those of my own parents in the hospital, were filled with love.

Beside me, the tearful smile on the Lord's face was too precious to describe. He was drawn into the night of his birth as I had been into mine. And I was gazing on Mary and Joseph!

A few moments more we watched in silence. Then the Lord turned to me.

"Do you see the angels?" he asked.

"I am beginning to," I replied. "Only barely."

He smiled as if he had a surprise for me. As indeed he did!

All at once the night sky exploded into light. Above the nativity, filling the sky around the hospital, a choir of what appeared to be a thousand angels was suddenly visible. The gorgeous sounds of their harmonies as they joined the carolers in *Angels We Have Heard on High* was unlike anything I had ever heard.

I watched in awe. I understood what the shepherds outside Bethlehem must have felt.

The carolers, however, took no notice of what was happening around them. After several more songs, their voices rose in triumphant climax with the angels. At last I grasped the full import of the familiar words. They were singing about heaven!

For lo, the days are hastening on, by prophet bards foretold,

When with the ever-circling years, comes round the age of gold.

When peace shall over all the earth, its ancient splendors fling,

And the whole world give back the song which now the angels sing.

As they sang, suddenly there was with the angels a great heavenly host praising God and singing, *Glory to God in the highest, and on earth peace among men.*

Then just as suddenly as it had begun, I found that we were back where my series of visitations had begun. It was no longer night. Christmas Eve was a memory.

I stood once again in front of my own church just as the morning service was about to begin.

FIFTEEN

Seeing and Unseeing

The Lord and I walked toward the church and were swallowed up in the crowd of worshippers.

I was in for another surprise. We were no longer invisible. People saw me and recognized me! Apparently they saw him at my side too. We approached the church as two ordinary men.

This could get very interesting!

A few of my acquaintances greeted me.

"Hello," said one, shaking my hand. "Haven't seen you for a while—how's everything going?"

"Good," I answered. "This is—"

I paused. Suddenly I realized the folly of what I had been about to say. I turned and asked, "How should I introduce you?"

"However you like," replied the Lord.

"Or...do you need an introduction at all?"

"It won't matter," He replied. "He doesn't know who I am."

I turned again to the man who had spoken to me.

"This is my friend," I said.

"Well, good morning to you," said my acquaintance. "It is good to have you with us. I am glad you could join us for worship today."

The two men shook hands. It was an incongruous sight. I expected some sign of recognition as their hands and eyes met. But there was none.

"Doesn't he know you?" I asked in surprise when the man was out of earshot.

"He thinks so. But his image of me exists only in his imagination."

I was astounded. The light from his eyes and the glow of love radiating from his face seemed so powerful as to be unmistakable. How could they not *see* him and *know* him?

As the stream of arrivals gradually moved toward the church, we fell in step, and entered the sanctuary to the sound of loud guitars and drums from a stage in front.

"Does *anyone* here know you?" I asked as we went.

"We shall see," he replied. "There are always those who recognize me. But sometimes they are not so easy to find. Ah...that lady over there, for instance," he said, nodding toward a woman in a wheelchair, "—she has sensed my presence already, but does not yet know what it signifies. I will speak to her before the morning is out."

"Will she know it is you?"

He smiled. "A perceptive question. Sometimes they know, sometimes not. Discerning my presence is not what many suppose. But the dear lady's heart will be warmed and she will not forget. All will be revealed to her in time."

He continued to glance around. "There are a few others here for me to seek as well," he said. "Unfortunately, not as many as there ought to be."

"But they are here to worship you," I said, incredulous that he should be like a stranger...*here* of all places.

"Actually," he replied sadly, "they are here for their traditions, doctrines, and emotions. Whatever image of me helps them do so to their own satisfaction—it is that image they venerate."

"It would shock them to hear you say such a thing."

"And it is a grief to me. But you are right—it would shock them indeed."

We took our seats. The service progressed. The Lord occasionally participated, such as when we sang a song of the Psalms. For the most part he merely listened. Two or three times I glanced over and thought I saw tears in his eyes.

When our pastor opened the microphone to the congregation, several came forward. I expected the Lord to take the podium and reveal himself. I thought of the incident at Nazareth when he rose to read the passage from Isaiah and then proclaimed himself the fulfillment of Isaiah's words. Why did he not do so again now?

He sensed my question.

"I *am* speaking," he said. "I am always speaking."

"Do you mean that you are speaking through those who have been addressing the church?"

"No, their words did not come from me. If they could hear what is stirring within the heart of the dear lady in the wheelchair, they would come closer to truly hearing from me than many of them ever have in their lives. But if she tried to express it, they would not perceive her deeper intent. She is a simple woman and slow of speech. They do not look for wisdom in such as her."

"What prevents them seeing it?"

"Their preoccupation with the beautiful, the charismatic, the outgoing, and the articulate. The Father's way is different. If I spoke out as you were expecting, it would not achieve what you hope. Only those who know my voice would recognize it. My words would but confuse the rest, or make them angry."

"Does our pastor know you?" I asked.

He smiled. "He is trying," he replied, and his voice was tender. "During one of these services, though I cannot say when, he will be ready. In that moment he will suddenly recognize me in his midst. At last his eyes will open. Then all the doctrines in which he is so bound will fall away, and he will know me indeed."

"Will you come here again?"

"I am always here," he nodded, "for those with eyes to see. I visit all the churches, though they are not my Church. I visit, and I wait. A few recognize me each time."

We rose, invisible to the eyes of the earthly worshippers, and walked down the aisle back toward the front doors of the church.

SIXTEEN

Mentor of Childhood

"A h," said the Lord, "here is one who has learned to see me."

A man stood waiting as we walked toward him. The instant I recognized him, the Lord disappeared.

"Sam!" I exclaimed.

With sudden embarrassment I realized I was shouting in the midst of the service.

"Don't worry—they don't know we're here," laughed Sam. "And it is wonderful to see you again too!"

I embraced my boyhood pastor affectionately. He had been dead many years, but I still thought of him often.

Everything inside was altered from a few minutes before. Whether this was the same service or whether time had passed, I had no idea. The congregation was again in the midst of a worship chorus.

I saw my wife in the same pew where she and I always sat. She was younger than when I had seen her in the courtroom. She looked much the same as I remembered her. She had obviously recovered from my death. She was dressed in bright colors and looked peaceful.

Gradually the singing ceased. The congregation sat down. I was curious to hear what the sermon would sound like to me now. I was one of those who had hung on our pastor's every word. Indeed, to many of us he was more than a spiritual advisor. We scarcely made a move in life without his counsel. It was our pastor who gave confirmation that we were in God's will and that our decisions lined up with Scripture. He was a man whose knowledge of the Bible we all revered.

I wondered if he would seem as wise to my expanding perceptions. As I was pondering what to expect, the congregation quieted. I could not take my eyes off my wife. I was so pleased with how she looked.

"It has been a year since you left her," said Sam beside me.

Slowly we walked down the center aisle. I knew most of the people seated on both sides of us.

We reached the front of the sanctuary and climbed the three steps to the podium. We stopped and stood next to our pastor who was preparing to begin his sermon.

"I remember this pulpit fondly," said Sam with a smile. "It was my first pastorate. Those were happy times."

"They were indeed," I rejoined. "I had many things to learn. I was so young back then."

"Weren't we all!" laughed Sam. "We had much growing ahead of us."

"From what I understand, we *still* have much growing to do."

"You have been speaking with the Lord!" laughed Sam.

I nodded.

"It is one of the first things he tells people here, to banish the idea of pearly gates with Peter standing at a turnstile checking to see who has an entry ticket and who doesn't. Those who envision sitting around on streets of gold with angels and harps are in for many surprises."

"Well," I said, "maybe *harps* are part of it."

"Yes," laughed Sam. "I know about that. For me it wasn't the music of a harp but a men's choir that ushered me in. But the principle is the same."

"A men's choir," I said. "How fitting. That was your specialty."

"You should hear our men's choir here! It is fabulous—fifty thousand voices strong."

"I can't wait!"

"I hope you will join us—you're a tenor, I believe. We're always in need of good tenors—especially on the chorus of *Wonderful Grace of Jesus.*"

"I love that hymn!" I laughed. "But I haven't sung in a choir for years!"

"What does that have to do with anything? Years is what we have. Eons! We have all eternity ahead of us. Peter had never been in a choir in his life. Now he is my assistant director when I am away."

"Peter is in your choir!"

"He never misses it. Speaking of St. Peter standing at the gates, it sounds as if that is the subject of today's sermon," said Sam as our pastor began. "Though as much as you respected him," Sam went on, "I am sorry to say that your pastor continues to miss the point of salvation."

Sam's words stunned me.

"He's not…" I began. "You're not saying he's teaching falsehoods?"

"I wouldn't go so far as that. But he is making the common mistake of reducing eternal themes to dogma rather than living truth. You will learn more about that later in connection with the Logos. Another of your dear friends, I believe, has been given the honor of explaining it to you. But as I was saying, your pastor would turn salvation into a one-time ritual rather than a moment-by-moment turning from sin. There is truth in his teaching. But it is a shallow representation of the high and glorious thing."

Sam's expression was tinged with sadness.

"But then I was exactly the same during my fifty years in the pulpit," he went on. "Evangelism was my life. I was so proud of being called an *evangelist*. I was obsessed with getting people saved by the formula. I paid far too little attention to the sort of people they were becoming in daily life."

"There is that word becoming again," I said.

"Nothing else matters."

"Not even salvation?"

"What is salvation if it is not becoming?"

"I don't remember hearing you preach such a thing."

"I never did. As I say, I was too preoccupied with the mechanics of salvation to recognize the importance of personhood. As you are discovering," he said. "I had to relearn most of my theology when I arrived here. I had to graduate from the formulas of Christianity to the living truths of Christlikeness. It was a shock to my system. But a joyous one. I have loved every minute of it!"

"I must confess to being confused," I said. "Does salvation not matter, then?"

"Salvation is everything. What is more essential than being saved from our sins? What *doesn't* matter are those tidy prescriptions we were so fond of—and that your pastor, God love him, remains bound to—that signify fulfillment of heaven's entry requirements. I am mortified to remember how proud I was of the people who went forward after my altar calls."

"I was one of them. I went forward right here," I said. "You baptized me up there in the baptistery. You were a wonderful spiritual mentor to me."

"I remember. And I treasured my friendship with you, though you were my son's age. You were a protégé to make a man proud. However, neither your going forward nor baptism saved you."

"What did, then?" I asked. "What *are* the entry requirements for heaven? Obviously I am here."

"There is no formula. You are not in heaven because of a prayer you prayed but for the life you lived—the man you allowed God to make of you."

"So being a good person *is* enough to get you into heaven?"

"Mere goodness is no entry standard either. That is not to dismiss the value the Father places on goodness. Goodness is of the air of heaven. Goodness is the energy of God's heart. The Lord is eager to welcome his brethren home with the words, 'Well done, *good* and faithful servant.' Yet the goodness that reflects the Father's character probes far deeper than what the world considers goodness. I am speaking of the man or woman who falls in with God's purposes, who lives by his will, who obeys what the Lord told us to do. Obedience to the Lord's commands is the only salvation. That is salvation indeed! Such is the *goodness* of heaven!"

"But who can do that?" I said. "No one lives perfectly by God's will."

"Salvation is not about perfection. It is about growing toward Christlikeness through obedient goodness. We are *becoming* God's sons and daughters. All so-called salvation that does not lead toward Christlikeness is no salvation at all. That's why some salvation prayers represent true salvation, because they begin a lifelong process of goodness-becoming. Other such prayers are eternally worthless. Or as we might have said back then, not worth the paper they're printed on."

SEVENTEEN

St. Peter at the Gates

A s Sam fell silent, my senses were again attuned to our pastor, standing between Sam and me in the pulpit so close I could touch him. He was already well into his sermon.

"…why we have devoted these past two weeks to the subject of salvation," he was saying. "It is all too common for people to assume that they will go to heaven, when in fact they have never actually prayed a salvation prayer. Thus they have not appropriated the blood of the cross to atone for their sins. They may be living a good life. They may even be in church every Sunday. Yet unknowingly they may be on their way to hell."

He paused to allow his words to sink in.

"We are all familiar with the oft-told story," he went on, "of the man who appeared at the gates of heaven and was asked by St. Peter, 'Why should I let you in?'

"The man replied, 'Because I have tried to live a good life.'

"'Sorry,' replied St. Peter. 'A good life won't get you into heaven.'

"A little surprised, the man tried another tactic.

"'I also went to church every Sunday,' he said. 'Sometimes twice a week.'

"'Sorry," said Peter, '—church attendance won't get you into heaven.'

"Further taken aback, the man tried a third time.

"'I prayed," he said, 'uh...*almost* every day.'

"'Sorry...prayer won't get you into heaven either.'

"By now the man was getting worried.

"'I was a faithful Catholic for years, before I converted to Protestantism,' he said. "I went through catechism and was confirmed. I must have said ten thousand Hail Marys.'

"But again Peter shook his head.

"'Being a good Catholic won't get you into heaven.'

"'I was baptized—twice actually...as a Catholic as a baby, and later as a Protestant.'

"'Neither will baptism.'

"'Let me see...I was in a Bible study. I know the New Testament pretty well. I believe all the Christian doctrines just like our pastor teaches.'

"'Sorry,' said St. Peter yet again, 'Bible study and scriptural knowledge won't get you into heaven.'

"'But I tithed and gave to missions and helped the poor in our community.'

"'Sorry,' said St. Peter one more time, 'tithing and charity won't get you into heaven.'

"Growing more than a little concerned by now, the man gave yet another answer. 'I was a good husband and father,' he said. 'I tried to be generous to my employees.'

"This time St. Peter merely shook his head sadly but said nothing.

"'What *will* get me into heaven, then?' the man asked.

"'Only one thing,' replied St. Peter. '—Repenting for your sins, praying a prayer of contrition, and then inviting Jesus into your heart. Did you ever accept the Lord into your heart?'

"'Well, I'm not sure…I don't suppose exactly in so many words. I thought that was covered by going to church and listening to the pastor pray from the pulpit.'

"'It is not covered,' replied St. Peter, 'unless you prayed to accept Christ, unless you accepted the salvation of his shed blood on the cross in atonement for your sins.'

"And thus the man was turned away from the gates of heaven."

EIGHTEEN

A Salvation Prayer

An expression of sorrow was evident on Sam's face. As the three of us stood there, heaven and earth occupied the same space. The two realms, however, were utterly distinct, with completely different logistics regulating two very different forms of life. Curiously, it was my pastor whose body appeared faint, filmy, ghostlike, while Sam appeared solid, real, strong, youthful, and full of vitality and energy.

"It grieves me to hear such talk," said Sam. "It is all so wrong. Yet I have no one to blame but myself for perpetuating such a distorted image of salvation. Dear old Peter himself prayed no such prayer. I have it from his own lips. The Lord never placed such a requirement on anyone. According to the standard salvationary formula and most church catechisms, none of the disciples would be saved."

Sam shook his head.

"The implications, when you think of it, are staggering," he said sadly, but with incredulity. "If you follow the salvation formulas that I myself preached for fifty years to their logical conclusions, all Jesus' disciples would be burning in hell right now. They never prayed what we called a sinner's prayer."

Sam paused and sighed.

"It is not often that one encounters anger here," he said. "One of the few times I have seen it was hearing Peter express his frustration at being trotted out in such settings as we are witnessing here with the *St. Peter at the gates of heaven* image. He becomes incensed at the folly of it. You know Peter, always one to speak his mind. He loathes being thought of as a celestial gatekeeper."

Sam let out another long sigh. "You can talk this over with Peter himself," he added at length. "I should not speak for him. He understands it far better than I do. He has been here much longer! You will meet him soon yourself. Actually, he is looking forward to seeing you."

"Peter is looking forward to meeting *me*!" I said in astonishment.

"Absolutely. Why shouldn't he be? Many saints new and old eagerly anticipate every new arrival. There were so many people from my own past waiting to greet me, and just as many that I was anxious to see. For years I had wanted to meet D.L. Moody and Billy Graham, only to find that they were lined up to see me! It was the thrill of a lifetime."

"I can't imagine what that was like for you."

"Everybody when they arrive has different men and women who have been influential in their lives that they want to talk to. That's why every homecoming and every reunion is so unique and happy...and surprising!"

"You can say that again!" I laughed. "The surprises keep coming."

"You're not through yet. There is an illustrious crowd of individuals waiting for their chance to talk to you. They are names you know well enough. Kelly, Woolman, Guthrie, Barclay, Weymouth, Laubauch, Kempis, Drummond, Clark, Lawrence, not to mention old Moses…even St. Paul—they are *all* waiting for their turn."

"I can't believe it!" I said. "St. Paul wants to talk…to *me!*"

Sam laughed. "He is most curious about some of your theories on his writings. He has been following your spiritual development for some time."

"Paul is aware of my ideas!"

"Keenly aware. You were wrong, he tells me, about the dating of the Corinthian correspondence—not that anyone cares about that anymore. But he loves your take on *Ephesians* and *Colossians*. He wants to hear more from your own lips."

"When will I see them all?"

"Everything in its time!" Sam laughed again. "Things here are ordained just as on earth."

Again our attention was drawn to the sermon in progress.

"And now," our pastor said as he moved toward his climax, "so that each one of you can be certain beyond the slightest question that you will not be turned away on that day when St. Peter asks why he should let *you* into heaven, let us all close our eyes. In the silence of your hearts, if there is any doubt in your minds whatsoever, simply repeat the salvationary formula after me."

My former minister paused. The church was silent. Every head was bowed, every eye closed.

"I must admit," said Sam from the other side of the pulpit, "this is too personal and painful for me. Let us be going."

Sam and I left the platform and walked slowly back down the aisle. Behind us, the minister's voice began to intone the familiar words, pausing often for the congregation to pray along. As he did, murmurs and whispers could be heard throughout the church.

"Dear Jesus...I realize I am a sinner...I know God's judgment is upon me...I deserve to be punished for eternity in hell...but I know that you died for me...you took my place...you took God's wrath upon yourself...you sacrificed yourself so that God's punishment would fall on you instead of me...through the cross you made atonement for my sins...through your blood I am washed white as snow...I repent and ask you to come into my heart...I invite you..."

I looked at my wife as we passed. I knew she was praying along. The sorrow I had seen on Sam's face entered my own heart. I realized that the pastor had accomplished little but filling my wife's mind with doubt about her salvation, as if her many years of living in obedience to the gospel meant nothing.

How desperately I longed to make myself heard. *"The Lord knows you too well for you to pray such words now in your life,* I wanted to say. *You are becoming. You are his child. The Father loves you."*

Yet I had to watch and listen in silence as she completed the prayer. I knew it would do her no harm. Seeing into its deeper significance, however, I realized what a misunderstanding of salvation it betrayed. I would have preferred hearing my wife pray in gratitude to God for their forty years together, rather than a prayer of doubt sown because of a salvation formula.

Already Sam was walking swiftly out of the church. I hurried after him.

"This spectacle behind us is heartbreaking," he said as I caught up with him. "Not a single soul is being saved. Nothing is being accomplished other than planting seeds of confusion in the hearts of the faithful, and false confidence in the hearts of the self-absorbed. But the obedient, like your wife, will grow beyond the formulas as you and I have had to do. Have no worries about her. She is God's daughter."

"And the self-satisfied?" I asked.

"Sad to say, they will continue to base their assurance of eternal life on the flimsy foundation of doctrinal correctness. A prayer such as this will actually do them more harm than good. It will divert their eyes from God's true priority in their lives. But the Spirit will never cease trying to break through. The fortunate among them will have their self-satisfaction shattered by painful circumstances."

"How will that help?"

"Pain and suffering are great aids in the birthing of spiritual hunger. Once self-satisfaction is replaced by hunger, growth begins. And blessed are those whose eyes open while there is still time to grow toward Christlikeness in their earthly lives. Unfortunately, many of them will not see these truths until their eyes are opened here. But God is good. He is the opener of eyes, whether there or here."

I pondered Sam's words as the church disappeared behind us.

I glanced up and saw a figure walking toward us.

"My time with you is at an end for the present," said Sam. "Your next companion will give you further insight into all this. I will see you again soon."

With that my former pastor and childhood mentor was gone.

NINETEEN

The Doctrine Library

The man who came walking toward me looked familiar in an odd sort of way. I was reasonably sure we had never met. Yet somehow I recognized him. He was dressed in what I would call old-fashioned attire, though such a phrase was meaningless here. It was perhaps that fact that caused me to think him a saint from an era former to my own, perhaps by several centuries.

He greeted me with outstretched hand.

"I perceive that you are struggling to place me," he said with a smile playing on his lips. "We never encountered one another in our past lives. You are more familiar with my ideas than my face. My name is John. I have come to accompany you on an important next step to your continued growth."

"Not…John *Calvin*!" I said in astonishment.

He smiled again, this time almost sheepishly.

"I am afraid so," he said. We turned and fell into stride together. "I would rather you simply thought of me as John. The Calvin carries much baggage I am still trying to shed."

I saw that we were drawing near a gigantic building. It easily comprised several city blocks and was twenty or thirty stories high. It was massively enormous, though plain and austere of design, constructed of gray cement block. Not a single window was visible. If I hadn't been in heaven I would assume it a prison. Yet people were freely coming and going from its front entrance.

"Here we are," said John, though it seemed presumptuous to think of him by first name. "This place is usually on the itinerary for new arrivals. Obviously it takes on unique features depending on individual need. I was chosen to give you the guided tour."

"It's immense! It looks as big as the Pentagon."

"Ah yes. We certainly had nothing like that in my time."

"It's not a very attractive building."

"No," smiled my companion. "You would be amazed how much different it looks to earthly eyes. It is considered one of the most beautiful buildings in the world. It is probably the most revered site in Christendom. Though here it includes all religions."

"What is it?" I asked.

"This is the Doctrine Library," he answered.

"A fascinating name."

"*Too* fascinating. Especially for one like me who thrived on doctrine in my former life. The contents of this building were a great snare to me."

"What is inside?"

"The first five floors are devoted to Christianity, the six floors above that to Judaism, and the rest to the other major and minor religions and sects. All their religious writings are housed here. This is the center for research and study and for the continual writing of articles and books innumerable."

"No wonder it's so big. Sort of like the old library of Alexandria."

"Intellectuals, teachers, pastors, priests, authors, and theologians of every possible religious persuasion come here to study. Thousands of sermons and homilies and Bible studies are churned out within these walls every week. Entire curriculums for Christian schools and colleges are written here. More post-graduate theses are researched and written here than you would believe— hundreds upon hundreds of thousands. The books that are produced would stagger your imagination. I spent my life here—my *former* life. But it is all a mirage. Its contents are mere wood, hay, and stubble. The entire library and all its contents will vanish in eternity like a wisp of smoke."

"Are you saying that we are only *imagining* it?"

"Oh no. It is real enough. But only *there*. No Doctrine Library exists *here*. The only thing dwelling within the walls of this building is discord, pride, and the vanity of intellectualism."

"Doesn't correct belief matter, then?" I said. "Doctrine *is* necessary, isn't it?"

"Oh, I suppose in one sense it matters a little," replied John. "When one dedicates himself to obey the commands of the Lord and his Apostles, it is important to believe with reasonable accuracy what they taught. But correct belief does not matter so very much. Obedience is the hinge upon which everything turns."

"Exactly what my former pastor said."

"Yes, we know about him. In the obedient heart, correct belief will always be revealed. It may take time. But willing obedience always yields truth. In the self-motivated heart, no belief is capable of being truly accurate at all. That's why belief in and of itself matters nothing. Obedience matters everything. Only obedience transforms belief into truth."

"So what about the ideas of faith? Are they important at all?"

"Only when enlightened by obedience. All too often, however, obedience is not the path that leads scholars to these doors."

"What does?" I asked.

"The pursuit of intellectualism. They are in love with their minds. Without the Spirit's illumination, however, the place is a desert. When you walk through its doors, you will feel the pall of death. What you thought when you first saw the building is exactly true—it is a prison. Yet untold thousands make this place their church of worship."

"Not literally their *church*?"

"Perhaps I misspoke. They turn what they find inside into the idols they worship inside their churches. I'm sorry if I sound unduly critical, but I was trapped in the deception for so long. I know I am responsible for its perpetuation in millions of Christians. Doctrinal orthodoxy was never as great a snare for you as for me. The moment you step inside, you will find the air of theological self-righteousness stifling. I would take a jackhammer to the place and reduce it to dust if it were up to me. But such is not the Father's way. He works good by his own ingenious and miraculous, though sometimes very slow, methods. Even in heaven I have to be patient."

"Why must we go inside, then?"

"It is intrinsic to our growth. We must never forget the deadness of doctrine."

"Surely it is not a snare in heaven?"

"You would be surprised. Speaking for myself, I visit this place regularly to remind myself what I was, to keep my priorities focused on what, by God's grace, I am becoming. Also because I have a job to do here."

As we approached, again I saw the white-robed figure of the Spirit standing beside the entrance. I wondered if it would accompany us inside.

"We can enter," said John. "She cannot."

"She?" I said in surprise.

He smiled. "He...*or* she," he said. "No one is quite sure. It remains one of heaven's intriguing mysteries exactly what we are to call him...or her. Much remains to be revealed. There is great discussion over the matter—good-humored discussion, of course. Not debate. Paul has some fascinating ideas on it. He has a theory that—"

He stopped himself. "It isn't time for that yet. Maybe when you have been here longer. Ask him about it. That man has a gigantic brain, and a heart to match!"

"Why can't the Spirit go inside?" I asked.

"He is barred entrance. The walls are an impenetrable barrier."

"Who blocks the way?"

"The spirit in control of the Library."

"What spirit?"

"The spirit of intellectualism.—But let us go inside."

Glancing back at the white celestial form standing in front of the building, I followed John through the wide double doors.

We entered an enormous and expansive entry hall. It was as big as a football field...*two* football fields!

"Is this just the lobby?" I said, glancing around. The walls were lined with more doors side-by-side than I had ever seen. "There must be two hundred elevators!" I exclaimed.

"There isn't room for them all in the entry hall," said John. "Many take the stairs up to the second floor to catch *their* elevators, some of the minor sects have to walk up to the third. Of course in my day there were no elevators, just many separate stairways."

"Why so many?"

"You don't think those from the various religions and denominations would *share* their elevator or stairs with those of differing doctrines? Every sect has its own which takes its scholars straight to their research facilities. They never speak to anyone outside their own belief system. Most find the entry hall challenging. From ceaseless practice they learn to keep their heads down while making a beeline for their elevator or stairway. Notice how quiet it is. As crowded as the lobby becomes, it is always deathly quiet. No one speaks until they are safely inside their isolated quarters."

"That is remarkable," I said as we strolled among the silent intellectuals. As we went, I perused the great variety of labels on the elevator doors—*Pentecostal, Anabaptist, Muslim: Shia, Judaism: Reformed, Presbyterian, Methodist, Judaism: Hasidic, Buddhism, Hinduism, Southern Baptist, Episcopal, Mennonite, Foursquare, Judaism: Kabbalah, Mormonism, Orthodox: Greek, Amish, Adventism, Orthodox: Russian, Judaism: Conservative, Anglican, Brethren: Open, Congregational Lutheran, Nazarene, Assembly, Regular Baptist, Conservative Baptist, Brethren: Closed...* and many more.

At the far end of the hall I saw two large double doors.

"Where do those lead?" I asked.

"I am embarrassed to have to share this section of the library with you," said John as we walked toward them. "Nevertheless, it is intrinsic to the tour. It is one of the largest research facilities in the building."

I now saw above the doors a sign reading *Calvinism.*

We walked into the room bearing John's name. Silence engulfed us. On every side the most erudite and somber scholarship was in progress. Men and women sat at desks poring over ancient texts. Others separated into cubicles were reading and taking notes. Vast bookshelves lined the walls. Many rooms dedicated to various aspects of Calvinist theology opened in a multitude of directions. Men and women were strutting about, many with huge Bibles under their arms and carrying thick notebooks, on their way to give lectures and teach studies that would showcase their vast knowledge of Scripture and Calvinist doctrine. Ponderous theological discussions in low tones were taking place in some of the rooms. As we passed, I caught snatches of familiar phrases I recognized all too well from having participated in the like myself.

Beside me John was silent. I could feel his grief. I knew he was praying as he went. If only these people who idolized him could see him now!

Gradually we made our way back into the lobby, then slowly to other floors. The atmosphere everywhere was the same. Study, discussion, analysis, writing, and note-taking were feverish. Every room evidenced the scripture, "Of the making of books there is no end..." along with Solomon's chilling conclusion, "and much study is a weariness of the flesh. All is vanity...all is vanity."

TWENTY

The Unity of Willing Hearts

W e emerged back on the ground floor. As we made our way once again across the expansive entry hall, we saw a man exit the door at its far end. He was apparently coming from the wing of a vast ground floor library on the opposite side of the building. Above the door, as we drew near, I read the word *Catholicism*.

I recognized him instantly. His face was beaming with childlike humility.

"It's John Paul!" I exclaimed.

"The very same!" laughed Calvin. After his somber countenance through most of our tour, it was good to hear him laugh.

John hurried forward and embraced the former pope with obvious affection. I was surprised when John Paul turned toward me with eyes of love.

"Hello, dear friend," he said. "It is a privilege to meet you."

"And for me to meet you," I said excitedly. "Though I wasn't a Catholic, I admired you greatly."

"There are no Catholics or Protestants here," he said. "Nor any other label. We are sons and daughters, nothing more nor nothing less."

The implications of what I had just witnessed suddenly struck me—the most influential Protestant theologian of all time embracing one of the most influential Catholic popes of the modern era. I glanced back at Calvin. He saw my expression of wonderment.

"The pope and I have become great friends," he said. "And not merely because we share the same name. The two of us get together almost every day to pray for the millions of souls trapped in the twin deceptions of Calvinistic legalism and Catholic ritual."

"You pray for all these people?"

"Absolutely," rejoined John Paul. "There is only so much we can do from here, of course, especially since the Spirit is prevented entrance into these chambers. But prayer has mighty wings throughout God's kingdom, as you will discover when you reach the prayer lake. So we do what we can."

"Here and there," added Calvin, "one soul, then another, then another begins to hear the High Symphony."

I glanced back and forth between the two men with question.

"Another of your friends will explain that to you," said John Paul.

"I admit, it is sometimes tedious work," sighed Calvin. "But all eyes will be opened. The only questions are *when* and *how*."

"And what means will be required to accomplish it," added John Paul.

"I speak from personal experience," Calvin went on. "Would that I had been more attentive to the higher themes of God's purpose far earlier. My growth and understanding would have progressed much more rapidly."

"We have both discovered that much has to be relearned here," added John Paul. "Most doctrines either fall away, or else are fulfilled in ways we never dared imagine. The only thing that does not fall away, as our friend Sam emphasized to you, is obedience. Theology evaporates. Obedience remains."

"You know Sam!" I said.

"Of course," laughed John Paul. "Everyone knows Sam."

"What matters is that one's heart is true," added Calvin. "True hearts learn rapidly here. Untrue hearts have a difficult time of it. Those who pride themselves on their correct beliefs, and assume that those beliefs qualify them for special treatment...they have the most difficult time of all. But God is constantly wooing hearts with his far off Song. Unity will triumph in the end, even over theology!"

"Amen!" added John Paul exuberantly. "It is only unfortunate that more of God's people do not discover the glory of unity and the bankruptcy of doctrine before coming here. Yet all eyes will be opened. Unity will come. Reconciliation marches forward to conquer the universe!"

TWENTY-ONE

High Walls

I left the Doctrine Library flanked by the two Johns. I was still awed to find myself in such distinguished company. Yet they treated me as an equal. From their demeanor, one would never guess them to be such revered saints of Christendom. The very idea of *esteem* here was completely inverted from its former meaning. Men and women were esteemed in heaven for much different character traits than was the case on earth—even in the church.

The gladsome jubilation of being with two men of such unassuming wisdom reminded me how many other "Johns" I was anxious to meet—especially in light of what I had just seen—from Edwards, Darby, Packer, and Piper at one end of the spectrum to Chrysostom, Bunyan, Woolman, and Newman on the other. Would they all be as enlightened, meek, and unpretentious as the two who were beside me at this moment?

Of course I was eager to meet John the great Apostle of Love most of all.

Oddly, the two Johns seemed *younger* than I was. Humble childlikeness was so thoroughly the defining characteristic of their nature that they were like two boys enjoying the day together. They were simply children of heaven.

As the three of us continued to chat like old friends, I began to hear singing.

On the crest of a hill about half a mile away I saw rising before my eyes two oddly constructed and singularly unattractive buildings. They sat next to each other, separated scarcely by room enough to walk between them. Considering the abundance of available land on all sides, this was peculiar in itself. Their shape, too, struck me as incongruous. Both were built like towers, reaching high into the sky. I was reminded of New York's ill-fated twin towers. Like the building we had just left, both were entirely without windows.

One of the two, constructed of beautifully hewn stone, was covered with ornate designs and carvings from top to bottom, culminating in an exquisitely elaborate series of towers, steeples, brightly painted domes, and decorated parapets and battlements and palisades, festooned all about with gold figures of what I took to be the apostles. Beside it, the second building of red brick was plain and austere without a hint of ornamentation. A more striking contrast it would have been difficult to imagine.

To further my perplexity, I realized that the singing I heard was coming from both buildings at once. As we drew nearer I recognized familiar evangelical hymns emanating from the building of brick, and chants of a mass from the stone cathedral. The closer we came, the more dissonant they were, as if the congregations of each were trying to drown out the other.

"It's not very pleasant music," I said wincing. "You would think they would make an effort to coordinate somehow."

The expressions of sadness on the two men's faces was so profound I thought they would weep.

"Sadly, *coordination* between the two houses of worship, as you put it," said Calvin, "is an anathema to both. It is the last thing either would agree to. *If* the worshippers in either church even knew the others were there," he added.

"What?" I said, glancing toward him.

"They come and go from opposite sides," he explained. "There are no windows. They are oblivious to one another. It never entered their minds in their former lives that any Christians but those of their own doctrinal persuasion would be allowed into heaven. Thus, their music makes dissonant noise to everyone from the outside who happens to hear it. They have no idea how repulsive it sounds. One never sees angels anywhere near the churches with high walls. Their highly tuned musical sensitivities cannot take it."

"Anything would sound better than this," I said in amazement. "What are these two buildings anyway?"

"Haven't you guessed? One is the church of Catholic Exclusivity, the other is the church of Evangelical Exclusivity. Obviously not all Catholics or evangelicals worship here. Only the most judgmental attend the churches of high walls."

"But this is incredible," I said. "They are so close together!"

"In almost every way they are identical, except, of course, in what they are trying to keep out. The conservatives are trying to keep out heresy. The liberals are trying to keep out conservatives. Their insular assurance that they represent the only path to heaven differs only in the specifics of their doctrines and rituals. But the spirit ruling both buildings is identical."

"What spirit is that?" I asked.

"The spirit of religion."

"And their walls," I asked, "why are they so high?"

"So they won't know the rest of us are here."

I stared back, stunned at his words.

"Their high walls enable them to preserve the illusion that they are the only ones in heaven," John added.

A long silence fell. I was timid to voice the next question that came to my mind. But I asked it.

"Are they saved?" I said at length.

"Speaking for the evangelicals," replied Calvin, "they are what they *call* saved. They are here, which is all they wanted from their Christianity. You get what you pray for. They prayed to get into heaven and here they are. Others, however, pray to become God's sons and daughters and they, too, are getting what they prayed for, though they certainly do not worship here. Some never prayed at all, and they are getting what they prayed for as well, which is nothing."

"Are those in these churches...*becoming*?" I asked.

"A perceptive question," smiled Calvin, "especially in light of the predestination and elect controversy precipitated by my writings. You have put your finger on one of the great paradoxes of heaven. It may be that *everyone* is predestined to become. All eyes are being opened. But the process is slower in some than others. So in one sense, those content in their churches of exclusivity have not yet embarked on the journey toward becoming. In another sense, however, the fact that such discovery awaits them signals that in God's economy it has begun indeed. God's beginnings in hearts is not always visible. We do not know all the stories of waking that may be taking place in those around us every moment. And as you see," he added, pointing to a translucent whiteness haunting both entrances, "the Spirit moves in and out freely here."

The former pope had said little during the recent exchange.

I turned to him.

"Speaking for the Catholics," said John Paul, "it may be accurate to say that those trapped behind those walls are in a purgatory of their own making. They think they are in heaven, because they are in church. Religion to them *is* church. It is the only frame of reference they know. They have not yet discovered the imperative of Christlikeness. Once they make that discovery, purgatory will vanish along with the high walls of their imagined cathedral. Then they will awake into the beginning of their salvation."

We turned and began walking away. The two Johns had had enough of the dissonance of disunity for one day.

I cast a final look over my shoulder.

"I see a few people leaving the buildings," I said excitedly. "They are even walking around and visiting with the others."

John Paul glanced back and smiled. "They are those whose hearts are yearning for unity," he said. "They are coming awake. They have begun to hear the High Symphony. The brotherhood of childship has begun."

"And now," said Calvin, "I believe there is one coming to meet you out of that wood across the way over there."

I followed where he was pointing. I saw the tall trees of what appeared a great forest. Between us and the forest lay a wide field. A man had just emerged from amongst the trees. He waved and headed toward us.

"We will leave you now," said John Paul. "Give our greetings to your friend."

"Who is it?" I asked.

"One you know very well," replied Calvin.

I left the two Johns and set off across the field.

TWENTY-TWO

Mentor of Youth

B ill!" I exclaimed the moment recognition dawned. I quickened my step and ran to meet my former neighbor who had also been the youth leader at our church. My father's friend had been a formative influence to my developing faith as a young man.

"I should have expected to see you!"

Bill laughed as we greeted one another with a fond embrace.

"Sam and I had a little argument about which one of us would get to talk to you first," he said. "That's not really the right way to put it. There aren't actually *arguments* here. A good-natured discussion, shall we say. We have both been very eager to visit with you."

"It is fantastic to see you!" I said. "I was sorry to be out of the country at the time of your funeral."

"What are funerals," rejoined Bill, "but testimonials to the past. They serve their purpose, I suppose. Those we leave behind need to put their emotions into perspective—*closure*, as it is called. But the reunions that take place here are so much better."

"So I have discovered! I am having a great time. The learning curve does take a little getting used to. I had no idea how many adjustments would be required to my outlook. There is more to heaven than I realized."

"You thought you would automatically know everything there is to know?"

"I suppose I did."

"So did I!" laughed Bill. "It takes us all by surprise—the discussions and questions and learning. Actually, you are progressing more rapidly than most. Some of what you and I need to talk about many don't grow capable of understanding for years. You're going to be ready for the High Mountains in no time—a few thousand years max."

"A few thousand years!" I laughed.

"The merest blink of an eye! It took me *ten* thousand," added Bill, laughing again. "I wouldn't trade a day of it for anything. How boring heaven would be if we weren't able to keep growing into ever more challenging ideas."

"It is invigorating!"

"It will keep getting better, believe me. All this is merely preparing you for the really important work of life in the High Places."

"My long discussions with you when I was young helped set my feet on the path of faith," I said. "I've wanted to tell you that ever since…you know, since you died. I can't thank you enough for your influence."

"Your insatiable spiritual hunger, your questions, your curiosity, were used in my life as well," rejoined Bill. "In your own way, you helped prepare me for my own growth toward heaven's high purposes."

"How did I help *you*?" I said.

"You were a bold thinker, even in youth," answered Bill. "That example was good for me. In all my years working with young people—of course, we're all young here!—I don't think I ever met anyone so curious about complex spiritual conundrums."

"It was my undoing!" I laughed. "Sometimes I was too curious for the comfort zones of my peers."

"I know all about that—how you were dogged by a reputation of being unorthodox," smiled Bill, almost humorously. "But that was only in the eyes of the *un*hungry. Spiritual curiosity is a greatly admired trait here. You had courage to think expansively about God and his ways. You are progressing quickly in your heavenly understanding because you trained yourself to think big about God."

"How *did* you and Sam decide who would meet me first?" I asked.

"We didn't. The decision wasn't ours to make. All things are ordained. It is our joy to fall in with the Great Will. And the two Johns needed to talk to you too."

"You know them!"

"We are on intimate terms with everyone. Also I was busy in my shop finishing up a project at the time. Sam was free."

"You have a woodshop here!"

"You bet. I couldn't live without my tools and projects."

"I can't wait to see it! There is nothing I would enjoy more than a theological discussion, as we used to call them, in your workshop."

Bill laughed at the memory.

"Theological discussions take on quite a different meaning here," he said.

"So I have noticed!"

"As does our work. You will be amazed at the hobbies and pastimes that keep you busy. Of course they aren't mere hobbies—everything one does here has eternal meaning. I am finishing up a cabinet at the moment for a woman in one of the mansions up on the slopes of the eastern—"

He stopped abruptly.

"I forgot," he added. "Have you been told about the mansions?"

"Not exactly."

"Ah well, time for all that later. And speaking of woodwork, from what I understand, you developed quite a shop of your own. You became a skilled woodworker yourself."

"I was never the craftsman you were."

"You made some very interesting things through the years. I watched over your shoulder for hours."

"You were there!"

"We come and go. That's part of the fun of life here. I loved visiting you in your workshop. You talk to yourself when you're working, by the way. Did you know that?"

I laughed. "So my wife tells me!"

"There were times I wanted to make a suggestion. But you know how it is—it's hard to make yourself heard. The two worlds merge, but they don't mingle. And we don't visit all that frequently. That's mostly the jurisdiction of the angels."

"Well, my woodworking efforts were strictly utilitarian," I said. "I was never able to achieve the precision of your work."

"Your dad and Loran and I spend a good deal of time in our workshop—we share it, actually. Some of the things we make...well, you will see for yourself. Creativity takes on such a high level here. One never knows what will be the result."

"My dad and Loran!"

"Sure. We get together almost every day."

"You live near each other?"

"Neighbors just like in the old days. Of course, everyone is neighbors with *everybody*."

"That's fantastic. Your houses are next to each other?"

"Not exactly. So much will come clear once the whole mansion thing is explained. Let's just say that the three of us remain very close.—But enough of all that. We will visit more in the workshop. Right now I am to explain a little more about the business of doctrine that the Johns discussed with you, and about the higher mathematics of heaven."

"I've never thought of heaven in relation to mathematics," I said.

"Mathematics is something you understand," said Bill. "It was one of your favorite subjects, if I remember correctly. The principle may also be explained in musical terms. Doctrine is simply the *mathematics*, or *music* if you like, of spirituality—the explanation of how spiritual principles function. Lower mathematics explains how the physical world functions. Here, the equations and theories are fulfilled. The algorithms of science, spirituality, and even music are governed by higher principles once they are infused with the life of eternity."

Bill paused. He seemed to be struggling for another analogy to illuminate the same principle.

"Think of it as a tapestry," he said at length. "It is the tapestry of the eternal history of the universe being woven by the hand of God. Man's earthbound eyes see only the back side of the cloth. Through the centuries men have expended great energy devising theories and equations and doctrines to explain the meaning of the universe—both physical and spiritual. But their search for truth is largely fruitless because they are analyzing with their intellects the threads visible on the reverse side—their colors and shapes and lengths and fabrics. Their efforts are governed by the mathematics of earth. And because infinite goodness and love are not the warp and woof upon which the strands of their theological reasonings are woven, the result is a jumble of confusion. They don't perceive what the Father is weaving on the other side.

"Doctrines and theologies analyze the back side of the tapestry. Theologians attempt to see God from the wrong side. They weave their theories on the strands of their own intellects, not on God himself.

"When we arrive here, we are led around to the front of the tapestry. At last we behold the glorious imagery God was weaving all along—the eternal purposes revealed by his character."

TWENTY-THREE

The Tapestry of Infinity

By now Bill had led me out of the field where we had met and deep into the forest of huge redwoods. It reminded me of the woods surrounding my boyhood home. I had loved nothing more than romping and exploring and making forts and climbing those enchantingly mysterious trees.

"I love this forest!" I exclaimed.

Bill smiled. "Memories of childhood?"

"Wonderful memories! My vision of heaven has always included trees like this, and recapturing the joy of those days."

"You will recapture it," said Bill. "Your future home—near mine, and of course near your parents— has a vast forest all around."

"Really!"

"You will be able to explore to your heart's content…just like you did as a boy."

"I can't believe it. That is too thrilling for words!"

"Heaven is childhood fulfilled. It is *everything* fulfilled!"

"What about Peter Pan?" I asked excitedly.

Bill roared with laughter. "You are referring to your childhood dream of being able to fly?"

I nodded.

"You will have to talk to Michael and the angels about that," replied Bill. "I know something about redwoods. But flying is outside my purview. Actually, though, it's something I'm waiting to find out about too."

We walked along under the spreading evergreen canopy of giants above us.

"Do you remember what the Lord said to you before," Bill began at length, "*Deep vision into the heart of things is one of the most important changes that comes with waking. You have made it, because you are making it.*"

I nodded.

"He was showing you how heavenly vision applied to people, allowing us to apprehend who they really are. The same principle applies to truth. Many look at the surface principles of faith with the same unseeing eyes with which they look at people."

"Non-Christians, you mean?"

"Certainly. But many within the household of faith are unseeing of eternal meaning as well. They are good men and women who *believe*, but whose vision of God's ways is superficial. They have not set themselves to look to *high* truth, to penetrate the *deep* meaning of spiritual principles. They satisfy themselves with the formulas of dogma. When they arrive here, the higher mathematics of God's expansive truths are difficult for them."

"There it is again," I said, "—the learning curve."

"Precisely. Truth on this side is larger than can be understood within the limited perceptions of earth. There we were able to grasp but shadowy hints. Here, all is brought into unity."

"It seems that a life of faith would prepare us for all this."

"It should. But look how great the adjustments are for you. It is more difficult for those who allowed their spiritual lives to be ruled by jargon."

"I see what you mean."

"They have no idea how thoroughly doctrines are turned inside out here. Terms like atonement, sanctification, justification, propitiation—they all fade almost into meaninglessness. They represent the terminology of the threads, not the truths of God's eternal Tapestry of Redemption. What the tapestry reveals is Fatherhood. The intellectual analysis endemic to nearly all theological systems simply cannot take in the high truth of an infinitely loving Fatherhood. But all eyes will be opened. All eyes *must* be opened."

We continued to walk among the great trees. I realized that it was no accident that we were here—among the giant trees of God's handiwork—as Bill explained God's *high* purposes.

"To grasp what I am talking about," Bill went on, "consider the concept of infinity. I'm sure you recall your old math professor, and how taken you were when you first encountered the idea."

"It fascinated me like few ideas ever had," I said.

"There was a great spiritual principle at work. That is simply that math principles have to be recomputed in infinity. The old equations don't work. Parallel lines in the old math never cross. In infinity, however, parallel lines *do* intersect. In the same way, once we reach spiritual infinity, the spiritual equations have to be recomputed. Many principles that seemed completely opposite to our former vision intersect here in heaven."

"Like heaven and hell?" I said.

"Perhaps. They are opposites according to earthly spiritual mathematics. Perhaps in eternity they will indeed intersect in some mysterious way few on earth can grasp."

"*Do* they intersect?" I asked.

"I don't know," answered Bill. "That is one of eternity's mysteries. But to complete the analogy," he went on, "heaven is infinity. You and I are now living *in* infinity. It is where all possibilities intersect and are fulfilled. Some of us call it Heaven's High Logos Truth. Here we enter into the heart of all things. Here is revealed the eternal Truth toward which earthly hints and shadows pointed—the eternal Word. The Truth. God himself. Here the glory of the Redemption Tapestry is revealed."

TWENTY-FOUR

The Symphony of Heaven's High Logos

"Let me tell you a little of my own story that you may not know," Bill went on.

"As a young man growing up in the church, when I began to be interested in studying the Bible for myself, I encountered a methodology of approaching Scripture that dominated the spiritual training I received.

"I look back with some regret—though that is a poor word, because we don't *really* have regrets in heaven—that I did not make more effort to discover the front of the tapestry. I should have known better. I was given hints that there was more to the story. In spite of the relentless indoctrination that goes with church life, I was occasionally uneasy about God's high things being explained simplistically. If I can change to the analogy of music, I would say that faint echoes were trying to break through into my consciousness of a melody from far away over the distant mountains of eternity. I sensed that I was hearing a symphony of more lofty themes. The explanations from church did not reach that Song of Eternity which began tugging at my heart.

"As I sat with my Bible in my lap, flipping through its worn and annotated books, scarcely a page without a note or underlining, it dawned on me that I might continue to study the Bible for the rest of my life and still miss the big picture of what God's Word truly *meant*...if I remained inattentive of that distant music filtering toward me.

"I knew I needed to climb to loftier outlooks in my understanding. I wanted to hear the composition as God meant me to hear it. What eternal strains and melodies was God sending through the universe as part of his grand heavenly symphony?

"You remember those days I'm sure," Bill went on with a smile, "That's when I began reading some of the old mystics and seeking deeper meaning in my walk with God. I shared some of those books with you. Yet I could never escape the confining bondage of doctrinal orthodoxy. The church pressure was simply too strong to believe just as everyone else did. I was too bound by the indoctrination to embrace the higher melodies. So even as I felt higher things and read of higher things, I continued to interpret it all through the lens of doctrinally correct orthodoxy. I could never break free to fully explore what I sensed was out there."

"I never knew all that was going on in you," I said.

"I kept it mostly to myself," said Bill.

"I went through exactly the same thing," I said. "It is difficult to embrace the symphony when everyone around you insists that the music you are hearing is in your imagination."

Bill nodded with a knowing smile. "Back in those days, if you stepped outside church orthodoxy, you got more than a slap on the hand. You were branded with a reputation."

"How well I remember!" I said.

Bill and I walked on reflectively.

"In learning to hear the music of Unity and Redemption in the universe—the Fatherhood-story—" said Bill at length, "we are progressively learning to see with high mountain vision. We are being prepared for life in the mansions."

"The mansions again!" I laughed. "When am I going to learn about the mansions?"

"All in good time. Just remember that the high truths of heaven cannot be quantified into a new dogma. We simply have to stand back and let the wondrous thing fill our hearts with wonder. We have to listen with awe to the High Logos Symphony of Heaven."

And as suddenly as most of my other interviews and discussions had ended, Bill was gone.

I found myself standing alone in the heart of the redwoods.

I was surrounded by a deep quiet. My heart was full of peace as only a redwood forest can bring.

Then faintly, far off, I thought I heard the distant strains of music. I cocked my ear, trying to make out the melody. But I could not quite lay hold of it.

Gradually it was gone. Again silence enveloped me.

Twenty-Five

Best Reunion Yet

I realized that I was alone for the first extended time since my arrival. Oddly enough for the many changes that had come to my perceptions, it gave me the chance to pause for a period of reflection.

Strange to say, with overwhelming evidence to the contrary, and in spite of the palpable *reality* of everything I had seen and heard, the thought again crept into my consciousness that I was dreaming.

Perhaps it was a natural response. Heaven was so different than any imagination could have prepared me for.

Looking back, I don't know exactly *what* I had expected heaven to be like. Every preconception had been turned upside down.

I suppose I had anticipated being constantly surrounded by people and angels and saints, as if everyone would be gathered in one place—a celestial church service of a hundred million people praising God together! Maybe deep down most people had been more influenced by Huck Finn's notion of heaven than they had any idea. "All a body would have to do there," Huck had said, "was to go around all day long with a harp and sing, forever and ever. So I didn't think much of it. But I never said so." I wondered how many Christians agreed with that assessment. I had certainly never considered that *solitude* and *learning* would be such integral aspects of it.

Now that I was here, however, discovering such unexpectedly wonderful new truths, I was enjoying myself immensely. It was the adventure of a lifetime...the adventure of eternity!

I couldn't wait for each new phase, each new revelation, each new conversation, each new guide who would accompany me in my journey.

This was heaven indeed—learning, growing, expanding, rejoicing...*becoming!*

Lying on my deathbed I had been thinking of questions about Noah's ark and Adam and Eve. The Lord was right—all those things had vanished from my mind.

As I strolled through the forest, suddenly I heard footsteps and a shout of greeting coming through the trees. I spun around and saw a young man running toward me with reckless abandon.

I call him a *young* man because he seemed younger than Sam or Bill or my parents or the two Johns. Nevertheless, I was aware of the visage of heaven about him. He was ageless. Contradictory as it sounds, however, he appeared younger than the others I had seen here.

I knew him the moment I turned. The sight bewildered me into speechlessness, yet filled me with more joy than it is possible to describe.

"Hey, Dad!" shouted my son with the voice of exuberance I knew so well. He was smiling broadly as he ran toward me. "Greetings, blessings, and peace!"

We embraced and held one another for the longest time.

"What in the world...how do you come to be here!" I exclaimed. I stepped back and beheld him in front of me. "Surely you are still alive! I only just arrived myself. Actually, I don't know how long it's been. It *seems* like only a day or two. Or...are you actually *here*? Maybe I am dreaming after all!

He laughed a great happy laugh.

"I am here, Dad," he answered. "I've been here for years—well, *aions* actually. You remember about aions?"

"How could I forget! You made quite a study of the subject."

"I made quite a study of *many* theological subjects," he replied. "Thankfully I am now delivered from my passion for theology. Yet the Lord works all things for good. Seeing how he does is one of the great joys of heaven."

"How can you have been here so long, and I just arrived?"

"Earth time means nothing here, Dad," replied my son. "Surely you have figured that out by now. Narnia, remember. Time sequences interweave."

"So time *does* exist here? They always said there was no time in heaven."

"Of course time exists here, but it works differently. It is never gone. Time here is like love. It never goes away. Spending it never uses it up."

"One of your other favorite subjects, as I recall—the *image of Love* I believe you called it."

He nodded with a smile.

"Time and love are indeed alike," he rejoined. "The more wisely you use the moments of eternity's time, the more you have."

"It is a riddle," I laughed. "Yet it is perfectly in keeping with everything else!"

"The main thing is that life here is not measured in hours, days, or years, but in *aions*—ages. Everything happens according to the appointed purpose of its unique age. Some aions last—to speak in earthly terms—a few minutes, others last a million years. But there is no parallel to the progression of an earthly calendar."

"Which is why you and I are meeting like this— everything upside-down?"

"You are in your present aion," said my son. "I am in mine. Their purposes may be different for each one of us. Actually, I outlived you—in our other life, I mean—by decades. Believe it or not, Dad, I lived to be over a hundred. But I have also been here for as long as needed to make progress in my ongoing journey just as you are in yours. I fully expect to find you as one of my needful guides at some point, when you will be instructing me and it will seem that *I* am the one who just arrived. In this case, however, the Lord sent me to accompany you to the next stage of *your* particular journey."

"I am glad he did! It is so great to see you! I have missed you!"

"And I you. After you died, there never was another with whom I enjoyed talking over ideas quite so much as you and I did. Iron sharpening iron, you know. My brothers and I got together a lot, of course. Yet what a privilege it was to talk over important things as a son with his father. Most people have too many issues with their fathers to be able to glean from them."

"You had some issues with me for a while."

"I am sorry about that, Dad. But we got over them. I realized that the issues were with *me*."

"You and I grew past that even in my time."

"By God's grace. Your own example helped me discover the imperative of the mirror—the key to all relational wholeness."

As we had talked, we left the redwoods behind us. We continued for hours, discussing many things. He explained his conversion to Orthodox Catholicism more fully than he ever had before, and how it influenced his spiritual pilgrimage. I recounted all the conversations I had had since my arrival, as he did many of his. He was envious—with a heavenly envy, which was equally delighted with my good fortune—of my having been met by the two Johns, as I was of his long conversations with saints Mark, Barnabas, and Pope Benedict.

When we parted, we both had tears in our eyes. We knew we would continue to see one another. From what my parents and Bill had said, I assumed we would be living near one another.

The extraordinarily joyous visit with my son left me with a great feeling of buoyancy and freedom. I was skipping along, singing my favorite hymns, feeling wondrously alive and jubilant and carefree, though the word seems an odd one to use under the circumstances.

Of course I had no cares. This was heaven!

Music was again in the air, even more distantly than before…too far away to be heard, only to be felt.

Gradually the sensation of hearing became intermingled with that of smell. I had already discovered that all the senses were connected here. Strange as it sounds, you could *taste* the music and *hear* heaven's fragrances. The sensation of "touch" had likewise been exalted to include *all* the senses. To *touch* anything—whether flower or rock or blade of grass or glorified human face—sent pulses of living energy through the ears and nose and into the heart.

I was therefore not surprised when I became aware that what I thought I had been trying to *hear* gradually gave way to the sensation of a *fragrance* of music. I realized that the air felt surprisingly moist.

I knew that animals were able to detect water from enormous distances. That same sense came over me now. I not only felt moisture in the air, its aroma penetrated nostrils and lungs with the sense of remembering something wonderfully nostalgic that I could not quite bring to the surface of my consciousness.

The terrain beneath my feet, like the air, began to change. The landscape altered completely from the coastal redwood forest. Soon I was climbing, not steeply but steadily, surrounded by conifers—fir and pine and cedar and spruce—and great boulders of granite.

I was in mountains now, walking at once through thick forests, then through high-plateau meadows full of grasses and wildflowers. Though the scent of water remained, with it was mingled the pleasurable aroma of warm pine needles underfoot. Streams and brooks flowed about me, their waters cold and clean and fresh.

I knelt down to drink from one of them. As the cool water trickled down my throat, hearing and seeing and feeling and tasting all exploded in my being into a wondrous sense of *knowing* inside my heart and brain.

I knew that I was drinking heaven's living water. I knew that the Lord had touched this water, just as he had the strings of the harp in the churchyard. I knew that it was imbued with God's Life.

I was filled with peace and quiet joy. I knew that my steps were being guided to the High Places, to the Father himself. My steps were ordered, my learning planned, my journey ordained.

I splashed the water from the living brook on my face, laughed in the sheer pleasure of it, then stood and continued on. Some time later I crested a high rocky ridge and stood, as I thought, at the summit.

What I beheld took my breath away.

TWENTY-SIX

The Prayer Lake

A vast lake, emerald green, oblong in shape, its surface like glass, spread out before me. I could just make out the opposite side some miles away. Above and behind the irregular shoreline rose ridges and mountains, forested, green, and lush. Their roots extended deep into the earth and drew their color from the emerald waters below. No more perfect harmony could be envisioned between an expanse of water and the living landscape surrounding it. The water was the life of every living thing.

The air remained warm and fragrant. As high as I thought I had climbed, the range surrounding me must comprise only foothills to higher mountains farther on. These could not be the *High* Mountains I had been hearing about. No hint of snow was visible anywhere—only the blue of the sky, the green of the trees, and the yet deeper green of the lake. The sun shone down with such warmth, in fact, that faintly perceptible heat waves shimmered off the surface of the water.

I descended a gradual slope toward the water. The lake was surrounded by pleasant beach in front of the trees rising behind it, though of what composition I could not immediately discern.

As I drew near the water's edge I saw that the beach was comprised of tiny stones, mostly flat, of many colors though generally light in hue, many perfectly white. Most were half an inch or an inch across. Some were smaller and others as large as two inches—all flat and polished smooth. They were so small and glossy that walking upon them was as pleasurable as on a carpet of sand. Tumbling together and knocking about, they made clinkily, stony, clattery music beneath my feet.

I stooped down, removed my shoes, then ran along the shoreline at the water's edge, splashing among the pebbles and water.

I could scarcely contain my exhilaration! What better than a lakeside on a perfect summer's day to epitomize the joy and exuberance of childhood?

I suddenly realized what heaven was. It was the opportunity I had often dreamed of—to be a child again with the mind and sensibilities and wisdom of an adult. It was the chance to regain the innocence, curiosity, inventiveness, and revelry of childhood, losing nothing that the intervening years had taught.

Yet the childhood of heaven was a new kind of childhood—an exalted, glorified childhood. In becoming the man I was intended to be, I had to become a child!

Heaven was so much better than anything I had imagined! If I wanted to stop and climb a tree, as I had loved doing as a boy, I could do so, as Bill said, to my heart's content. If I wanted to run splashing and laughing into this very lake and swim all afternoon, what was there to prevent me?

In the distance, I saw a woman at the water's edge,

walking barefoot among the pebbles away from me. She paused every so often and picked up one of the small stones.

She was moving slowly. I came up behind her and fell into step at her side.

She glanced toward me and smiled—a quiet, peaceful smile. She did not seem surprised by my presence. The expression on her face was sheer contentment. There was no other place she would rather be. She was exactly where she was *supposed* to be, where she *belonged.*

The instant the thought entered my mind, however, it also occurred to me that she was different than anyone I had yet encountered here. She bore traces of age—a few strands of gray hair, the slightly wrinkled skin of a fifty year old. I had seen such signs of age on no one else, not even centuries old John Calvin. Everyone had been youthfully ageless. The woman seemed real enough. Yet it occurred to me that perhaps she was not actually dead, that I was seeing her still alive, that she was not fully *here* yet.

She reminded me of the harp lady. Her eyes reminded me of someone else, too—someone I had seen recently, though I couldn't quite place it. I could not escape the sensation that she was still alive on earth, yet was aware of her heavenly surroundings. Was it possible that she was alive in both realms at the same time?

"Yes, this *is* where I belong," she said softly in answer to my unspoken question. Her voice, like her countenance, was full of gentleness. "As one becomes accustomed to God's ways, *place* as well as time flows in fluid harmony with his purposes. You will find that neither are easy to define by mortal standards. I am certain you have discovered by now that the rules change here."

"I am trying to get used to it!" I laughed.

"All things here are fulfilled. You are now *inside* the equations of earth's physics, in the same way that you are *inside* the ideas of earth's theologies. I believe one of your friends told you all about it."

I nodded.

"Because you are inside them, you are learning to see all the way into them. The principle is equally important in order to understand prayer. That's why I mention it. In all things, we must move beyond former explanations to get inside heaven's truths."

Again she paused, stooped to pick up another pebble between her fingers. After examining it a moment she gently replaced it where she had found it. She moved on. I strolled along beside her, drawing in deep draughts of the mountain air.

"You are looking for the prettiest pebbles, I take it?" I said.

"Oh no," she replied. "Nothing so dull as that. I am looking for live souls who need praying for."

"*Live* souls? I see nothing along this beach but rocks."

She smiled. "They are much more than that," she said. "Get down on your knees and look closely."

She dropped to her knees and plunged her hands deep into the smooth, wet, shiny pebbles at the water's edge. I knelt beside her and picked up a small stone and turned it over. I was astonished to see a name written on it.

Mary, I said aloud.

I looked at another…then another…and another. All had names inscribed on them.

Armando…Denver…Catherine…Lisel.

I grabbed a handful and examined them all. On every one was written someone's name!

Margarita...Hans...Lek...Halah...Carol...Patrick... Alfredo...Robert...Nancy...Ivan...David...Enrique... Masud...Christopher...Tabitha...Gregory...Susanna... Tarik...Julio...Otto...Robin...Timothy...Kama...Ramon... Rebecca...Alison...Elizabeth...Jeremy...Luke...Karl... Calandria...Matthew...Louise...Marilyn...Mandisa... Chang...Jurgen...Peter...Margaret...Clonia...Miquel... Anna...Nigel...Omar...Alexander...Chanda...Janet... Hashim...Gerda...James...Douglas...Diana...Eloise... Jimena...Zelig...Jacques...Richard...Esther...Amira... Kim...George...Shamir...Joseph...Caresse...Masud... Kyeong...Petrov...Manuel...Sabina...Catalina...Svetlana. ..William...Adara...Bedwyr...Rashida...Joan...Rachel... Meshel...Mark.

I glanced up and around the lake. Stones like these surrounded the water everywhere.

"There must be millions of them!" I exclaimed. "Who are all these people?"

"Millions of men and women and children who have been prayed for, and who still need praying for. There may be a billion...even a zillion!" she added, giggling with delight.

"How can that be?" I said.

"It's not so hard to believe when you think how many prayers people pray for one another."

"I see what you mean. People are constantly praying for their friends and loved ones."

"The lake is full too," said my companion. "Its depths are filled with more stones than anyone but God can count. They extend so deep that only he knows how deep the stones go. They go all the way to where heaven and earth meet and come out the other side. Every stone is a prayer someone has prayed for the loved one whose name is written on it. God remembers *every* prayer. He will answer them all in the right time."

"What are you doing, then?"

"I am praying for the ones that come to me, the stones I am given to pray for. They are the people who need me to pray for them. God will answer the prayers, but he needs us to participate in his answers. Sometimes it is our prayers that give the stones wings to return to earth as answers."

"I don't think I follow what you mean."

"The prayers are sent to God's prayer lake for safekeeping. Here they are nurtured, cared for, polished, and more prayers added—prayers of the angels and saints, more earthly prayers—"

"And *your* prayers?" I suggested.

"Yes," she smiled, "and my prayers. This great prayer lake exists in the Father's heart. Some of the stones remain here for many years, who can say why, until the time is right. Other prayers are answered more quickly. Some are buried deep in the midst of thousands of other stones where they are ground about in order for their rough edges to be worn smooth and ready for God's purpose. The Father knows what is best, and always does what is best, and only what is best."

"How do you know which ones to pick up, which ones out of the millions you are supposed to pray for?"

"I trust the Spirit to guide my hand. Sometimes I sense that a stone I have picked up is not ready for my prayers and I set it down again. Most of the time as I read the name someone has written as a prayer request, a sense comes over me what I am supposed to pray. If not, I merely lift the name into the Father's care, knowing that he knows the need and will see to it in his time."

"What a wonderful calling," I said.

"Prayer is indeed a noble calling. Especially as we learn to pray according to the Father's purpose. I never pray my own prayers, but only what the Spirit would have me pray."

As she said the words, I saw the white figure of the Spirit hovering behind her.

"One thing we must never do," the lady went on, "is get in the way of what the Father desires to accomplish in another's life. It is one of life's most difficult lessons, seeing and feeling the burdens and sorrows and heartaches others must bear in their journeys to brokenness. Mostly I pray that God's purposes in every life would be accomplished in his perfect time and in his perfect way."

"Are the people you pray for still alive...on earth, I mean?"

"I don't know," she answered. "I am not given to know. I have been given to pray for them, to pray that God's work will be done in their lives. I think some are already here. But an occasional heaviness in my heart tells me that many are also still on the other side."

She paused and grew thoughtful.

"There is one I have prayed for recently who is troubled. I sense that his story and yours will soon join. It may be that the Spirit will lead you to his stone."

TWENTY-SEVEN

Souls Take Flight

The prayer lady stooped and picked up one of the largest stones I had yet seen. Slowly she turned it over.

"*Warren*," she said slowly and reverently. She closed her eyes and her lips began to move imperceptibly. Her prayer lasted but a moment. She opened her eyes and smiled.

"A long life," she said softly. "A life of difficult growth...of hard-won becoming. Long and memorable and..."

She paused. A hush came to her lips. She held the stone tenderly between her hands, almost caressing it, then closed her eyes again. After a moment she opened her hands and held them aloft, palms to the sky.

Suddenly with a noiseless flutter, some winged creature—a butterfly yet so much more than a butterfly, a beautiful live soul taking flight!—flew out of her hands. It soared into the blue above. Its wings grew wide and white. Within seconds I was beholding a great radiant dove, the perfect likeness of a soul set free, returning to its eternal home.

She gazed after it in wonder. Tears of joy fell from her eyes. I looked at her hands. They were empty. The stone had disappeared. It had become a *living* being, God's child, and had winged its way into the heavens.

"It is not often I am privileged to see the answers take flight so visibly," she said softly and with a full heart. "Most of the answers winging homeward are not so easy to see as the glorious transformation we have just witnessed. Many of the answers steal upon those to whom they are sent on invisible angel wings. Many remain unaware even when the answers come."

Suddenly I heard a far-off chord, though not from a harp. It sounded like a vast orchestra. It was followed by singing…distant, faint, but huge and full as if from ten thousand voices.

A sudden gasp and expression of wonder came to the woman's face.

"It is the angels!" she whispered. "The angels are singing. The dear man Warren must just have come home! The angels are rejoicing to welcome him!"

"And look!" she exclaimed, pointing in the distance. A burst of light had just appeared over the mountains. I followed her hand and saw two men walking side by side bathed in white. "That must be him now! The Lord has met him and is beginning to explain the transformation."

She turned away. We began walking back in the direction from which we had come. She seemed to sense that the holy encounter we had just observed was too personal to intrude upon.

We walked a good way in thoughtful silence.

"Are you… still alive… there, I mean… or are you dead, too?" I asked at length.

"Here… there… alive… dead," said the woman, repeating the words with a smile of knowing on her lips. "Have you not yet learned that all meanings are

different now? I am where I am. I am where he has placed me, doing what he has given me to do."

We made our way further beside the lakeshore. She resumed picking up one stone at a time, looking at the name, smiling, then breathing a few words of silent prayer. Afterward, she gently placed each stone back where she had found it.

Following her example, I began doing the same.

We continued on, drifting apart along the shoreline, each about our prayerful business. With every stone I picked up, I was filled with sensations that enabled me to sense how to pray. I knew that the Spirit was imbuing my prayers with the Logos of his purpose, exactly as the Lord had promised his disciples he would. What a privilege to participate in the important business of heaven, lifting the prayers of earth, imbued now with God's Spirit in them, into the Father's heart.

I picked up a non-descript gray stone. I turned it over and read the name. Again, I seemed to know what to pray.

When my lips were stilled, I set the stone down among the others where it had lain. I saw the woman approaching. Almost disappointed, I realized that the time for its winged flight was not yet.

"You are part of that man's story now," she said with a smile.

"I sensed that," I replied.

"Do you see that there is much work to be done here," she asked, "—important and eternal work? Many lives remain in the balance."

"I am beginning to see it," I said.

"What is to be accomplished is not only the perfection of your own childship, and mine, but our contribution to the growing personhood of countless others."

"In other words—childship is both personal and mutual?" I said.

"Exactly so," smiled the woman. "That prayer stone was given life by your touch. It had lain in the lake, infusing into itself the emerald waters of life, awaiting this moment. Someday you will meet that man whose life will be changed by the answer to the prayer you just prayed. You are helping others—some here, some still there—into their eternal childship, even as you are growing into yours."

"Is there a stone with my name on it?" I asked.

"Of course," she rejoined. "There were many prayers lifted up on your behalf through the years. Most of them have already flown back to their home."

Suddenly across the lake I heard a plunk and a splash. I turned toward the sound in time to see a tiny stone disappear into the depths of the emerald water.

"Another prayer?" I said.

"Your wife just prayed for you."

"She *still* prays for me?"

"Of course, every day."

"But I am already here. What prayer could yet need to be answered in my life?"

"The prayer of all prayers—that you will be all that God purposes you to be."

Again I looked across the water. "Now that I think about it, this lake seems strangely familiar," I said.

"It is the mirror image, upside-down, if you like, of one of your favorite lakes. You and your wife visited it many times. If you look carefully, you will be able to make out the reflection around the edges of many people standing staring down into the water."

"I do see them! Of course—we honeymooned here. Do those people realize we are here?"

"While still in the flesh, they do not sense that

heaven is all about them, and that the inhabitants of heaven are in their midst. Once here, of course, as you have discovered, the two realms intermingle freely."

"Is this lake then, the repository of all the world's prayer stones?"

"All the prayer stones from every garden pond or hospital garden or wishing well or lake or stream or river on earth becomes a live prayer stone here, a sleeping prayer awaiting its metamorphosis and return to earth to accomplish its eternal purpose."

"How can such a lake—even in heaven—possibly contain all the world's prayers?"

"You speak in contradictions!" laughed the woman. "Have you forgotten where we are? There are no limitations in heaven. This lake is not merely of unfathomable depth, it is of *infinite* depth. It is capable of containing all the prayers that have ever been prayed."

I laughed as I absorbed the stupendous thought.

"But it hardly needs to do that," she added "As many new prayers as are being dropped into all earth's prayer waters every day, answers to earlier prayers are flying up and homeward. Prayers are coming in and answers going out constantly. If you look carefully, you will see many answers leaving the lake even now."

I gazed out across the water. My eyes gradually focused. I saw that what I had taken for heat waves rising off the surface were in truth millions of tiny white butterflies emerging out of the emerald waters and flying colorfully back into the lives of those for whom their prayer answers were intended.

The prayers that had been sent to heaven were being sent back to earth as answers on the tiny spirit-wings of God's messenger angels.

And with the revelation, I was left alone.

TWENTY-EIGHT

City of Gratitude

My steps led me away from the lake. With a full heart and much to ponder, I was soon descending out of the forested mountains. I found myself meandering through a pleasant wood of birch.

I wound through its trees of delicate white bark, widely spaced, a soft carpet of fallen leaves at my feet. In stark contrast to the vibrant spring greenery from the environs of the lake, I seemed to have walked straight through the summer months and arrived in this wood in the midst of Fall. The trees were alive with the glories of yellow and red and gold and orange on their slender white branches, leafy flowers ablaze on woody stalks. The air smelled different too—rich, dry, earthy, autumny.

I was following the hint of a path, though it was not well-defined. I did not think where I was bound next. I simply continued where the path took me.

My heart was full. Every exchange, every renewed acquaintance, every conversation expanded my consciousness in more ways than I could absorb.

For some reason I found myself reflecting on a sermon our pastor had preached about paying one's debts. He had quoted the parable of the unforgiving servant along with the required due of the uttermost farthing. He focused more on hell than heaven, and on the debts of sin. In his economy, God was the great judge and jailor of eternity.

Curiously, I now found myself thinking about other kinds of debts—good debts, happy debts to pay. It occurred to me that perhaps God was not a judge demanding payment, but rather a heavenly Banker who made provision for every possible debt in the universe to be stricken from the books and paid in full.

What debts might *I* still owe? Were there debts to be paid in heaven as well?

Suddenly names and faces and images flooded my mind. My heart overflowed with love as one after another was brought to my remembrance.

All I could think was how thankful I was for each one, how I cherished them and loved them, how God had used them in my life in large ways and small.

Suddenly I realized that the debts I needed to discharge were debts of *gratitude*! The very thought caused my heart to swell.

The moment the profound revelation was borne upon me, the way I had been following became more pronounced beneath my feet. Moments later I came to a fork. In front of me the path split in two directions.

I stopped and let my eye drift along one, then the other. In the distance to my right I saw a large city on the horizon. A signpost at the intersection pointing toward it read "City of Gratitude."

An arrow pointed to my left in the opposite direction, toward what looked like a range of foreboding mountains. Its sign read "City of Debt."

I turned toward the former. As I began walking again, the wood receded behind me. As far away as the city had seemed, I quickly found myself entering it.

The place was modern and bustling. People were coming and going. It did not take long for me to recognize it as the town on whose outskirts I had grown up. It was a shock to my sensibilities to leave the peaceful birch wood and find myself again surrounded by the pace of urban life.

The first person I saw walking toward me, beaming with the joy of a thousand filial emotions, was the woman who had given me life, my mother. She was even more beautiful than I remembered her from our brief meeting after my waking. No wonder my dad had fallen in love with her!

"Mom!" I shouted as I broke into a run toward her.

I scooped her up in my arms as if she had been a child and swung her around in the air. She giggled with delight.

"It's great to see you by yourself," I said, setting her down in front of me. "That was a big crowd before! We hardly had a chance to visit."

"We will have plenty of time," she said. "I can't wait to have you over to our mansion. I think you'll love how I've fixed it up. Yours will be practically next door...but then *everybody* lives practically next door!" she added with another laugh.

"That's what Bill said."

"You've seen Bill?"

"We had a long visit. I never knew he was so fond of mathematics."

"Everyone's knowledge increases exponentially here. You would be surprised how much there is to learn...about every subject you can think of."

We fell into step together.

"There is something I have wanted to tell you for years," I said at length. "I always regretted I didn't tell you before you died."

"There is time for everything."

I smiled. "Do you remember all that trouble I had in school when I was young," I said, "when the other children made fun of me and bullied me and called me cruel names?"

"How could I forget? It so grieved my mother's heart. I wished I had never made you change schools. That first year was awful for you."

"It got better," I said. "Actually I have fond memories of the later years. But I wanted to tell you about something you did that had a lifelong impact on me. Whenever I came home with stories about being made fun of or called names, you told me to pray for my classmates, especially the ones who caused me the most suffering. What a lesson to teach a young boy—to return evil with good! I want to thank you for that, and to express my gratitude for being the mother you were."

"I made mistakes."

"Whatever they were, I've forgotten them. That's all in the past. You raised me to be a boy, then a man, of character. What is more important than that? I could not be more grateful."

"Thank you."

"There was also the influence of your compassion for people. Your heart was so giving and tender to those in need...the elderly people you ministered to...those young and old you took into our home. You were a woman of compassion and I learned to honor that. It was one of the most treasured legacies a mother could give a son."

My mother's eyes closed briefly. She simply nodded in humble acknowledgment of my words.

"Now that I think of it," I went on, "there was also the time…"

As we walked along together, many more instances came to my mind for which I expressed gratitude. It was as if a dam had burst inside me, unleashing a great torrent of memories. All were now imbued with the miraculous healing touch of gratefulness, appreciation, and a thankful heart. With every word of thankfulness, something released inside me. As gratitude flowed out in a flood, love flowed back into me in a yet greater flood! I also told her about my experience in the Maternity Ward of the hospital. She said she had had a similar experience after her arrival watching her own father and mother.

How long my mother and I walked and talked, happily sharing memories, it must have been an *aion*—the purposeful aion of thanksgiving.

Gradually it dawned on me that everyone we passed was staring in our direction.

"Everybody seems to know me," I said.

"Of course they know you!" laughed my mother. "This is our home town. And it is your City of Gratitude. They are all people you will want to talk to."

And so it was. I owed every one a debt of gratitude—some I owed dozens, even hundreds.

What a joy it was to pay those debts. I had never felt such liberation and joy as came from saying *Thank you* for words and gestures, for smiles and encouragements, for exhortations and challenges, and for the multitude expressions of love large and small that had been shown me through my life. With every encounter my heart filled yet more. Gratitude was a door standing wide for the entrance of the great Love of the universe.

My dad and I also had a long talk together, if possible even more filled with thankfulnesses. My sisters came next. What a joy to reminisce and laugh with grateful hearts over so many mutual memories of growing up together.

I then met childhood playmates, people at church, my parents' friends in whose homes I spent so much time.

I met the woman who had given me my first job pulling weeds in her garden.

I met every teacher from every school.

I met classmates ranging from kindergarten through graduate school, surprised with every encounter by the myriad gratitudes that filled my heart to express.

I met the pastors and coaches and youth leaders who had helped mold me.

I hardly noticed as the city changed while I made my way along. It became the city of my adult life where my wife and I had gone to college and lived and worked and raised our family and grown old together.

I now met college friends and business colleagues and friends and acquaintances of my adult years, even those with whom I had had conflicts and disputes. Yet now, by the wonder of heaven's miracle, I knew that I had gratefulnesses to discharge to them as well.

Everywhere—in stores and houses and schools and hospitals and offices—were men and women, children, teen-agers, young and old alike—to whom my heart went out in thankful gratitude for the contributions, large and small, ongoing or momentary, they had made to my life.

The conversations that took place were as varied as the individuals themselves.

"There was a day when I was stressed and burdened by terrible pressure," I said to a lady known in our church as a prayer warrior. "I didn't know it at the time, but I recall the incident now with the eyes of eternity, and I see you watching me and sensing my anxiety. I see your eyes close and your lips moving in silent prayer for me. I thank you for listening to the prompting of God's Voice on my behalf."

"One evening during my college days," I said to a former college acquaintance, "I was dreadfully depressed, feeling worthless and lonely. You went out of your way to talk to me. It was but a brief moment. But that you cared enough to turn aside and share a few words with me made a great difference to me. Your kindness told me that perhaps there was something worthwhile in me after all."

And on and on they went...to try to recount them more fully would take a hundred books...

"Do you remember when I was going through severe financial struggles and you..."

"Do you remember when I was in the hospital and you were one of the nurses on duty..."

"Do you remember the time I was discouraged about the future and you prayed for me..."

"Do you remember the day you were ahead of me in line at the grocery store and you let me..."

With each debt of gratitude discharged, I knew that I was growing inside. The Spirit had led me to the City of Gratitude that I might be expanded in order more fully to thankfully know the Heart of God.

Twenty-Nine

A Man and His Arduous Journey

Having made my way through the city from one end to the other, I left it from the opposite end.

Spreading out before me was the mountain range I had noticed when standing before the fork at the two signposts. In their midst, though a long way off, I saw a man coming toward me. My eyesight must have improved far beyond 20/20. Though I could faintly make him out, he was a *great* distance from me…miles away—perhaps hundreds of miles. Steep hills, valleys, ravines, and treacherous pits of unfathomable depth extended between us. The mountainous rocky desert was altogether forbidding. I had seen nothing like it in all my time here. Smoke trailed up from several open canyons. The fissures appeared volcanic, extending deep into the bowels of the earth, like burning sores on the landscape.

I shuddered. I wasn't sure I wanted to keep on in this direction. No hint of green was visible. Unconsciously my steps slowed.

I continued to eye the man. I couldn't be sure from such a distance, but he was apparently attempting to hail me. How he would succeed in traversing the dangerous terrain between us, I could not imagine. I felt like Lazarus gazing upon the rich man with an impassable gulf between them.

Whoever he was, he kept bravely on. As I watched, over and over he disappeared behind a cliff or deep into a ravine, then reemerged. This went on again and again. Each time by degrees he drew a little nearer, before disappearing again, then yet again coming back into sight—walking, climbing, occasionally falling, but always picking himself up and trudging on. I could see that his hands and knees and elbows were bruised, skinned, and bleeding, and his clothes tattered from what must have been a lengthy journey.

As I watched, my heart went out to the man. If he was trying so hard to reach me, struggling mightily against all the odds that would prevent him, the least I could do was make it easier by shortening the distance.

I began walking again, hurrying now in my desire to help the poor fellow.

I set out across what had appeared such impassably precipitous terrain. The moment I stepped forward into it, however, the ground beneath my feet changed into gently rolling grassland. The change continued with every step. The inhospitable desert gave way at the touch of my feet, and was transformed into the rich panorama I had become accustomed to since my waking. I found myself walking along at the moving vanguard of an amazing transmutation—behind me the lush landscape of heaven, in front of me and gradually being swallowed up as I went, the wasteland.

I hurried on, anxious now to reduce the rocky distance between myself and the man.

He saw me trying to ease his arduous journey. He must have been aware of the transformation of the land resulting from my approach. He began running even faster, as he was able. Boulders, gorges, and steep climbs still separated us, however, and prevented him making as much progress as I did.

Gradually we came near enough for me to make out his features. I thought I might recognize him. Yet I was certain I had never met him.

He crested one last crag out of a bottomless pit. With its smoke clinging to him as he emerged out of it, now seeing me close at hand, he came running toward me.

For the first time, I saw that between him and me lay a small lake. After his superhuman trek, I assumed he would be parched beyond belief and would stop for a drink. But he ran around it, limping and struggling with clumsy effort, skirting the water's edge. He came straight for me.

"At last...at last," he sighed in desperation. "I have searched for you everywhere!"

"Where have you come from?" I asked.

"From the City of Debt. You were the one person in the world I most needed to see. But I could not find you. I have been looking for you for a thousand years. At last my search has been rewarded!"

With the strange words he fell into my arms, weeping like a child. Unlike anyone else I had yet met here, his were not tears of joy, but of sorrow and remorse so bitter he seemed unable to endure it.

I was completely bewildered. He obviously knew me. I had no clue who the man was.

I comforted him as best I could. I was limited in what sympathy I could offer, however, in that I had no idea what was the source of his grief, or the reason for the burdensome weight he was carrying.

He wept and wept in obvious anguish. By degrees the passion of his outburst subsided. Haltingly he made an effort to speak.

"I am so sorry," he said. "I am sorrier than I can express. Can you possibly forgive me?"

In complete perplexity I returned the earnest gaze of his pleading eyes.

"I beseech you," he went on, "if there is the tiniest compassion in your heart, please forgive me. I beg your forgiveness for the years I stole from you. Please release me from the prison of my guilt."

"I am sorry," I said. "I am at a loss to know how to help. I have no idea what reason I have to forgive you at all."

A great wail burst from the poor man's mouth. He broke again into uncontrollable sobs. It was a misery I had known few times in my life to witness such abject agony in a human soul.

"Don't you understand!" he howled. "It was *me!* I am the man who shot you. I am your murderer!"

Instantly I remembered him from the courtroom.

He fell to the ground before me, groveling on his face. His body was heaving in such an anguish of torment I thought it would consume him, and that he must die on the spot.

The seconds that passed as I stood gazing down on his prostrate form—an *aion*, perhaps, as my son might say—filled my mind and heart with emotions indescribable. Whatever ideas of vengeance may occur to the fleshly old man, whatever doctrines rise from the wellsprings of the lower nature, when confronted with true heartfelt repentance from another of our kind, the divine humanity of our higher nature rushes to the surface in a mighty flood.

I knelt beside the weeping form. Gently I laid a hand on his head.

"My dear man," I said tenderly, "my heart is filled with forgiveness, and with the love of Christ. It was there from the moment it was required. Take and receive. Forgiveness is yours in abundance. Rise and let God heal your guilt, and make you whole."

I set my other hand on his shoulder. His whole frame quivered beneath my touch, trembling in mingled relief and disbelief.

Slowly he turned and sat up. His face was wet with tears.

For the first time since I had seen him, a smile crept to his lips. It was a smile of hopeful gratitude, and dawning joy—slow to break forth in the lingering remnants of incredulity—that his long quest had been fulfilled.

His was the tearful smile of a child.

I offered my hand. He took it and I pulled him to his feet.

Strange to say, in that moment I felt like a father to him. My forgiveness had birthed a renewal of life within him.

I took him in my arms and held him for an aion. It was the aion of his healing, and the beginning of his childship.

At last he stepped away. At his side I beheld the vaporous filmy light of the Spirit's presence. The man's eyes sought mine. Their expression was again one of entreaty. When he spoke, it was in scarcely more than a whisper.

"But…will *he* forgive me?" he said.

"He will because it is through him that I forgive," I replied. "His forgiveness fills the air of creation. It is all around us waiting to rush into our hearts. He is your

Father. He created, therefore he restores. He heals, therefore he redeems. He loves, therefore he forgives."

"But how…what must I do?"

"Simply breathe in the air of eternal Fatherhood that is about us and in us. Then ask of him what you will."

"But how will he hear?"

"He is everywhere. This is his universe. He hears all. His Spirit is beside you at this moment."

At the words, the man fell on his knees and bent his face to the ground.

"Lord Jesus…God my Father!" he cried. "Forgive my great sin!"

THIRTY

Waters of Wholeness

A t the words of repentance, the Lord was beside us. I backed away.

The Lord embraced the man who was weeping again freely, then led him down the gentle slope to the rich green waters of the small lake. He walked into the pool, leading the man by the hand until they both were waist deep. I saw no river or stream flowing into it. Yet I knew that these waters had come from the prayer lake in the mountains. And I knew the man now entering them at the Lord's side had been prayed for by many, one of whom I knew would have been my wife. I was witnessing the fulfilled culmination of those prayers.

The Lord turned to him and spoke a few words. I could not hear what passed between them. The man again burst into tears. A radiant light glistened from his eyes and face. The Lord laid one hand on his chest, the other on his back, then gently eased him into the healing waters of restoration.

When he lifted him out a moment later, all around a vast choir of angels broke into song. I spun around with wonder.

Angels surrounded us everywhere. The music they made contained all the melodies and harmonies of every hymn of praise I had ever known.

As far as I could see, the rich green landscape of heaven reigned. No sign remained of the rocky burning waste of pits and canyons. Hills and forests and streams and lush meadows filled the vision in every direction. Goodness had triumphed not only in the heart of the lamb who was lost and now was found, but also over the very ground beneath our feet! The mountains and hills rejoiced with the angels!

As the angels gave song to their praise, the Lord led the man out of the waters of his baptism. He beckoned to me. I walked to the water's edge to meet them.

"These are the Waters of Wholeness," the Lord said, speaking to both of us. "All must drink of these healing waters. These are the waters from whence spring the Life of the High Mountains. All eyes must be opened, all breaches healed, all sins forgiven. Therefore, drink. Drink of the Waters of Wholeness. Because you forgave," he said to me, "your brother is forgiven. Because I forgive, you have forgiven. Because the Father forgives, creation is made whole. Redemption is nigh."

The Lord stepped back. I knelt in the blue waters with the man beside me.

We both bent our lips to the cool waters of Life, and drank deeply.

I felt the liquid blue of revelation fill all my senses as had the fragrances of my walk through the foothills up to the lake of prayer. I smelled, I tasted, I heard, I *felt* the water spreading through my body and bloodstream, into every vessel and pore, and into my soul.

When I lifted my head, the music ceased. The Lord and the angels had disappeared.

I was alone with the man whose eternal fate was so bound up in my own.

As of one accord we rose, left the Waters of Wholeness, and began walking together. Neither of us spoke. Not only were our hearts full from the import of what had taken place, we sensed as well that a crossroads of yet mightier import lay ahead in our respective journeys.

The joy of reconciliation did not come without a price. That price the Lord had paid. We were about to enter more fully into the reality of it.

Ahead in the midst of the lush panorama loomed a single rocky peak. It shot up out of the verdant countryside as an anomaly in the landscape, solitary and menacing. It was both near and far, at once unassailable, yet I knew that we must scale its cliffs.

At the very apex rose two empty crosses of wood. A shudder coursed through me.

We reached the base of the strange monolith. Again I saw the path beneath our feet coming to a fork.

We stopped and looked at one another. Different destinies were marked out before us.

I took the path to the right, my companion that leading left. We parted toward opposite sides of the slopes and set out.

Thirty-One

Garden of Secret Prayer

Moments after I was alone, again my surroundings changed.

I found myself climbing a narrow path out of a valley behind me. I could not see to the top, but it appeared to be a hill of moderate height outside a large city spreading up the other side of the valley. It was not the same small mountain at whose base the man and I had parted. Yet I knew that my steps would lead to that peak in time.

The air was hot and dry. Dusk was settling over the dusty landscape. As darkness descended, campfires came into view scattered about the mount.

I continued up the winding way. Soon I came to the outlying region of a grove of bushy trees. Their gnarled trunks spoke of antiquity, though most were not much taller than my head.

Subdued voices came up behind me. Somehow I knew their conversation to be in Aramaic, though I understood every word.

Instantly I recognized the voice of the Man leading the way.

"Abide in me…" he said. "I am the vine…he who abides in me bears much fruit."

It was the Lord speaking to his disciples!

The timeless words were so familiar. Yet suddenly I was hearing them for the first time. They plunged to the depths of my soul.

I stepped off the path, listening as the voices came nearer. The darkness steadily deepened.

"As the Father has loved me, so have I loved you," the Lord was saying. "Abide in my love. If you keep my commandments, you will abide in my love. These things I have spoken to you that my joy may be in you, and that your joy may be full. This I command you, to love one another."

Twelve robed men walked slowly by, led by the Lord himself in his earthly body. Neither he nor the eleven took notice of me beside the path. They seemed unable to see me.

Moments later they disappeared into the depths of the garden. I hastened after them.

As I came into the grove, I was able to make out tiny fruit among the small silver-green leaves and branches. At last I knew them for olive trees.

By the time I reached them again, the twelve had stopped. The disciples were seated about the ground talking quietly. A few were lying down.

I wandered about trying to find where the Lord had gone. Within minutes, heavy breathing and soft snoring replaced the conversations. All eleven disciples were asleep.

Somewhere deeper in the depths of the garden I heard a voice. It was no more than a whisper. I moved toward it.

As I came upon him in the dim light, the Lord's back was turned. He was on his knees. A luminescent light hovered beside him.

Then came the whispered words, faintly audible, that I knew so well:

Abba, Father, all things are possible to you...yet not my will, but your will be done.

I was in the presence of one of the holiest moments of history. The anguish in his expression was palpable. I tried not to breathe. The garden was silent.

At length the Lord rose. His expression was worn, his face drenched with sweat and stains of blood.

He returned through the trees to where the disciples were sleeping.

When he was gone, I took a few steps forward to where he had knelt to pray. The white transparent Presence had remained at the holy seat of relinquishment. I knew it was there for me.

An inner compulsion drove me to the ground in obedience to the Lord's example. I felt my knees settling into the imprint of his in the earth. I knew his prayer was mine to pray as well.

"Abba, Father," I whispered, "Not my will, but your will be done."

As I uttered the words, my body trembled from head to foot. Solitary as were my surroundings, I knew that I was kneeling at the crossroads of history, at the dividing line between heaven and hell, at the eternal locus between life and unlife.

I was in the presence of the Godhead—Father, Son, and Spirit.

Though seemingly alone, I had never been less alone in my life. I was encompassed round about with the creating Love of the universe. By my secret prayer of self-relinquishment, I had entered into the essence of his threefold Life.

I rose. A great change swelled through my heart. I had relinquished my will into the Father's. Henceforth, in all ways my personhood would be rooted in and fulfilled by his will. My own personal *I am* would forever be defined by the childship of my knees resting in the imprint of the Lord's in the lonely garden altar before the Father's throne.

I turned to leave the holy place of relinquishment. I knew that the salvation of the world had been won. The Lord's sacrifice had been made in this secret place by the abandonment of his Will into the Father's.

I had entered into that salvation in my former life. Now I was privileged to participate in the higher reality toward which its shadowy earthly form had pointed.

To know salvation from the heavenly *inside* crowned my heavenly sojourn. I was re-living what I had lived before, though no longer through a glass darkly. Out of my former life, I entered into the higher Logos which lay at the heart of all former revelations.

My heart overflowed with thanksgiving that revelation was ongoing, even that salvation itself was ongoing, and that life eternal would continue to deepen and expand forever.

Praise filled my heart for the opportunity to pray again the timeless expression of childship, *Not my will.*

THIRTY-TWO

Just Sentence

I emerged from the inner sanctum of the garden. The disciples were awake. I was jolted back to the reality of the earthly present.

Angry voices echoed in the darkness. A minute later the light of torches bobbed in the night. A mob led by a contingent of soldiers entered the garden.

All this time no one had taken notice of me. As with my previous encounters in the earthly realm, I was invisible to those on the other side.

Suddenly a light flashed. The next instant I was among them, seemingly in my fleshly body. The protection of heavenly invisibility evaporated. All eyes turned toward me.

"It's him we're after," shouted the captain of the Roman guard. "Seize him!"

A dozen soldiers ran up, pushing and shoving. They struck me alongside the head, then bound my hands.

"What are you doing?" I cried. "I've done nothing wrong!"

"You've done *everything* wrong," rejoined the captain angrily. "There are so many witnesses lined up to condemn you we haven't been able to interview them all. You'll get a trial all right. But it's the cross for you."

"The cross!" I shuddered.

"Your treason is a capital offence."

With his words, they dragged me out of the garden and down the hill toward the city. The eleven disciples scattered for their lives.

Only the Lord was left. The mob took no notice of him. As the soldiers pulled me along, he walked at my side. His presence and the calm expression of his countenance were reassuring. I assumed he would speak on my behalf against the witnesses they said were lined up to accuse me. At his word, they would surely release me.

I arrived in the city and was subjected to the mockery of a trial. The whole city came out against me. Any hope that anyone would speak in my defense was shattered. The Lord stood quietly by, invisible to soldiers and crowd and lawyers and priests. I waited for him to intervene, to stop the proceedings, to order my release, to tell them, however grievous my offences, that my sin had been washed away. Yet he spoke not a word.

At last I was given the opportunity to offer a defense. The Lord turned to face me. His eyes bored straight into mine. I remembered his own example before Pilate and the chief priests. I remained silent.

Seeing that I refused to defend myself, just as the captain had predicted, I was condemned to death.

Standing in the dock, mocked by my accusers, the Lord stood with me as the decree was announced. Tears of Love fell from his eyes and he gazed upon me. As his eyes probed mine, I knew that my sentence was just. I deserved nothing less. I had not been falsely accused or condemned. I acknowledged that justice had been rendered unto me. I received and accepted it. Death was my appointed fate. My deserved fate. My just fate.

By mid-morning I was struggling along, a taunting and accusing crowd clustered close on every side. I was dragging a rough-hewn cross of insufferable weight. Back, shoulders, feet, hands, and arms were blistered and bleeding. I staggered out of the city, whipped and kicked if I slowed. Step by inexorable step I drew closer to what was called the Place of the Skull, the dreaded site of crucifixion.

I realized that I had begun my climb to the top of the cross-crowned hill.

As the Lord walked along beside me up the hill of Calvary, no thought of escape now entered my mind. Escape would have been impossible had I tried. The pain was unbearable. But I did not resist it.

THIRTY-THREE

Hill of Salvation

We reached the summit. Soldiers cut my bonds and set the cross on the stony ground.

"Lay down on it!" commanded the centurion of the guard.

The Lord walked forward and stood before me. At last he spoke.

"Would you like me to take your place?" he said.

His words stunned me.

"But...*you* do not deserve to die," I said.

"No. But my life is not my own. I love you and would be willing to die in your stead."

"I could never ask you to do such a thing."

He smiled, as if I had answered well. "Then, my brother," he said, "let us die together. I will die to show you how to die."

I stared back, trying to absorb the magnitude of what he had offered.

"You would do that?" I said slowly. "You would share my fate?"

"I would do all, I would move heaven and earth, I would die myself to enable sin to be conquered within you."

"I do not deserve such a sacrifice of love."

"We will not speak of love deserved. No love is deserved. All love is deserved. Love *is*, and that is all. You are my brother, a son of my Father. Therefore I choose to give my sacrifice of love."

I could but bow my head in humble thanksgiving.

"The eternal sacrifice is always mutual," the Lord went on. "Thus does the Father perform the miracle of the Ages. I will example death for you. I will enable you to die unto yourself. In our mutual sacrifice, we will make Life alive."

My eyes were wide with awe. The wonder of revelation overwhelmed me. At last I understood the needful and *personal* imperative of the cross.

Now," he said softly, his words heard by no one in the universe but me, "—obey as you have been instructed. I cannot do this alone. My power over sin requires your participation to effect full reconciliation. Take your place on the cross."

I could do no other than trust him. To trust and obey him was life, even if it meant death. I *did* trust him. I would now trust him for my life, my being, my salvation. As I had trusted him in life, I would trust him in death. All remaining doubts, questions, and fears were swallowed in trust.

I knelt and laid my back on the longer of the two beams.

"Stretch forth your arms," said the Lord. "Lift your hands to receive the executioner's nails. Lift them to the Father. You are in his care now. He will allow nothing but good to come to you. Though you are slain, you may trust him."

I did as the Lord said. I stretched out my arms on the beam, then lifted my hands. As I did so, I whispered a prayer.

"I am yours, Father. I yield my all into your Love."

Above me the centurion stepped forward. He held a great hammer in one hand, huge iron nails of crucifixion in the other. His shadow fell upon the cross.

Beside me I glanced over and saw a second cross lying on the ground. Upon it lay my forgiven murderer. I knew he had climbed Calvary's hill on a different journey than mine. The red of blood stained the ground beneath him. The expression in his eyes as he glanced toward me was impossible to describe. He too lay on his cross knowing the sentence against him just.

No sooner had I noticed him than my attention was drawn again to the Lord at my side.

He stooped down, then did the unthinkable. He lay down on top of me. His back settled upon my chest, his legs upon my legs, his feet upon my feet.

Whether we were two physical bodies or two heavenly bodies, I could not tell. I only felt his presence sink down *into* me until his very being was inside me.

His words resounded in my memory: *Abide in me, and I in you.*

The warmth and peace of indwelling oneness was all in all. I was still me and the Lord was still the Lord. We were two. But we had become a mutually abiding union of wholeness. As he lay on the cross over me and in me, our beings merged into one.

He stretched out his arms over mine and lifted his hands to the Father. I heard him whisper, "Abba, Father, into your hands we commit our spirits."

The centurion bent down. He set a great nail to one of the Lord's hands, then drove it through his flesh.

A ghastly cry of anguish echoed from the Lord's mouth. I felt his body tremble in agony. But as the nail pierced his hand, squirting his blood over my arm, then stabbed through mine into the wood of the cross, I felt nothing.

Another nail followed through our other hands, with the same result. Then our feet. The Lord's blood spread over my body and seemed to permeate my whole being. I felt his blood washing me cleaner than I had ever felt.

But the Lord over me and in me and through me absorbed all the pain. Nothing could touch me.

With the final nail binding our hands and feet to the cross with no means of deliverance, lightning flashed above us. A peal of thunder crashed and shook the earth.

I felt myself falling...tumbling...twisting with strange forces swirling above and about and through me. Blackness engulfed me and overwhelmed even my awareness of its blackness...and I knew no more.

THIRTY-FOUR

Mentor of the Silence

M y rudimentary knowledge of science had acquainted me with that great mystery of the universe which physicists described with the term *black hole.*

No one knew what a black hole was—only that beyond their boundaries the rules of physics ceased to function with predictability. Time meant nothing, space, energy, light, motion, gravity...such terms no longer carried meaning. Light was sucked into a vacuum of nothingness. Theoretically time might even go in reverse. Inside a black hole *everything* was turned inside out.

Now that I was here I realized that in heaven the rules and algorithms and doctrines changed in exactly the same way.

Yet heaven was the reverse of a black hole. It was the infinite *light* hole, where the light of the universe makes all things whole. Heaven was the *Light Whole* of beginnings, endings, and all things between, where all time and life were consumed into the great Oneness of the universe.

In theorizing about black holes, the scientists had unwittingly approached the threshold of heaven itself. Their only blunder was in mistaking for "blackness" what was in truth an Infinity of *Light*—God's Light.

When moments later, therefore, I found myself walking in broad sunlight, I knew that somehow I had been transported through a supernatural heavenly wormhole out of death into light.

The two crosses, Calvary's hill, the ordeal of crucifixion, even the Lord himself, had all disappeared. Wherever I was, and whatever sequence of time, or *untime*, was in operation, I had emerged out of the blackness of my second death.

I did not long ponder the time warp into which I had been drawn out of the events just past. I saw that I was about to be met again. Using a word of limitation such as "past" is utterly incongruous. Especially if I was inside some time-suspended reality in the midst of heaven. No past or present existed in eternity. Everything that was happening would continue to live within me as an ongoing *now*.

Fittingly, I was about to encounter the man from whom I first learned the principle of the Eternal Now. His wisdom in apprehending that the timeless *now* of eternity could break continuously into the *present* of earthly existence had exercised a profound impact on my spiritual growth. His emphasis on hearing and obeying the impulses of God's Voice had set the orientation of my spiritual life for more than six decades of earthly existence.

Two men came walking toward me. When I saw them in the distance, however, they were engaged in such vigorous dialogue I wondered if they would walk by and take no notice of me.

I recognized the younger of the two from the photograph on his book. Again I speak in contradictions. Both were of that timeless heavenly age I saw on nearly every face here. He was only younger in the sense of having lived more recently and, as I recalled, having died as a young man. He was dressed in what would be called a business suit, as befitted his earthly profession as a college professor.

The face of his companion was unfamiliar. Yet instinctively I knew him to be the well-known eighteenth century tailor of Mount Holly. He wore the plain linen garb of farmer and shopkeeper, both of which vocations had been dear to his heart. His head was crowned, which at first glance struck me as unusual, with the customary wide-brimmed hat for which early Quakers were known.

The professor was grilling his mentor with questions. The moment I saw them I was anxious to do the same. I was well familiar with the writings of both men. It was the professor's book, however, more than any other, that had set me seeking deep truth as a young man.

I rushed forward to greet them.

"I have been hoping to see you!" I said enthusiastically to the professor. "Your book changed my life!"

"My *book*?" he said with a curious expression.

"Your testament of devotional writings."

"Ah yes. Occasionally I forget that they made those essays of mine into a book after my death. You know what they say," he added, chuckling, "they ignore you in life and make you famous after death."

"I am glad they did. I must have read my copy ten times."

He laughed with innocent delight, the joy of existence seemingly ready to overflow its bounds.

"Your writings about center-living focused the priorities of my life," I added. "I cannot thank you enough."

"I am pleased to have played a small part in your spiritual development."

"You set my feet on the path toward the Center, toward obedience as the objective of faith."

His next response took me by surprise.

"It wasn't me who set your feet on that path," he said.

"Who, then?" I asked, glancing momentarily at the old Quaker at his side who stood with an expression of contented quiet.

"It was *you*," answered the professor. "I did nothing more than focus your *own* spiritual hunger in directions you already wanted to go."

"How could you know that?" I said.

"I followed your life-story," he rejoined. "It is one of the things we do here—we follow life-stories and help boost them along in what limited ways we are able from this side. Perhaps I gave you a few insights that assisted you in your journey. However, don't forget one of the Lord's first teachings—*Blessed are those who hunger and thirst for righteousness, for they shall be satisfied.*"

I nodded.

"You hungered to be good," he went on, "to walk with God. You desired to order your life by the Lord's commands. The few thoughts in my book that meant so much to you would have accomplished nothing had your own heart not been hungry for righteousness. It was *your* hunger, not *my* book, that made the difference."

"I see what you mean," I said. "That brings up one of life's greatest curiosities to me."

"What exactly?"

"Spiritual hunger. Where does it come from? Why is one person hungry to grow spiritually and another is not? Why do not *all* men and women hunger for righteousness? It seems that that is what we are made for."

"It is indeed. But your question is as old as Cain and Abel."

"I see what you mean. Yet it puzzles me how two individuals can be influenced by the same factors, be taught the same principles, read the same book, face the same circumstances...and yet respond entirely differently.—By the way," I added, "have you met Cain's wife?"

The mentor of my young adulthood roared with laughter.

"Troubled by that historical conundrum, are you?" he said. "No, I haven't actually. Like you, I am looking forward to it. There are many I am anxious to talk to. But we have all eternity before us. Perhaps you and I shall seek her out together."

"But why *do* some men and women want to live Godly lives," I persisted, "while others are uninterested in the spiritual themes of life?"

"There, my friend, you have put your finger on the question of the ages. Why do some hearts turn to their Creator, while others seek only to gratify their own desires? It is one of life's deepest mysteries."

"You have been here longer than I," I said. "Have you discovered the explanation?"

"Let me just say that the answer is in the process of being revealed. I am still learning. The Father will complete all life-stories. His resolutions are more difficult, and obviously take longer, in those who did not follow their implanted spiritual inclinations during their earthly lives. Spiritual hunger assumes different characteristics here. Many forms of inner awakenings are revealed. I rejoice, however, that you were one who followed your spiritual yearnings to their rightful Source. You set your feet early in the direction of your heavenly Home."

"The *Source*," I repeated. "Are you speaking of what you called the Center?"

"Source...Center...Home—it matters little what we call it. It is where everything leads—even within black holes, or as we prefer to call them, as has already been revealed to you, *Light Wholes*. We are bound on an eternal journey back to our origins—to the Heart of life-creating Fatherhood."

"And that is what you meant by the Center?"

He thought a moment. "The journey takes us forward and back in time," he replied, "and through all the stages and aions of life, for He is all in all. But you are right—I called it the *Center*. That was not a term of my own invention. But as you discovered, it was a helpful orientation."

THIRTY-FIVE

Toward the Center

How well I remembered the words from the man's book.

"Deep within us all," I said, quoting from memory, *"there is an inner sanctuary of the soul, a holy place, a Divine Center, a speaking Voice, to which we may continuously return. Eternity is at our hearts. Yielding to the Light Within is the beginning of true life. It is a dynamic center which illuminates the face of God. Here is the slumbering Christ, stirring to be awakened. He urges us to an amazing Inward Life with Him lived joyously from this Inward Center."*

"The words sound familiar," my companion laughed. "Did I write that?"

"You did," I replied. "I always identified the phrase *Life at the Center* as epitomizing the life of a Christian. I must confess, however," I added, "I never felt that I had fully apprehended all it was supposed to mean."

"How could you when you were in the flesh? It was a process of growing *toward* the Center. While yet bound to earth we cannot apprehend everything the

Center means. We do not find the true Center until we are here. It is the Home our hearts long for. Here too, however, only those whose hearts hunger for the Source of Life experience the purifying flames of the Center."

"Not everyone in heaven discovers the Center?"

"I don't know. I would hope everyone does in time. But the journeys of our heavenly steps, as formerly, are dictated by hunger. Many arrive wanting merely to enjoy heaven's blessings. They are not aware, nor would grasp the high truth if you told them, that the business of heaven is no different than the business of earth—to grow in intimacy with the Fatherhood. Life with the Godhead is not static. It is continually enlarging. But it can take time for hunger to be felt, even here. You saw the two churches with high walls."

I nodded.

"Most of those who isolate themselves from the brethren have not yet begun the journeys to their appointed and imperative Destiny."

"Will they?"

"In time. One, now another, then another, quietly leaves the constricting fellowships of the unhungry. You saw them. The high walls must first be torn down in their own hearts. As those walls disintegrate, their eyes are opened. Fatherhood takes hold. Hunger sets in. Their journey to the childship of the Center has begun. But the journeys here, and the growth and learning that take place, are infinite and varied according to individual need."

"We are in heaven," I said. "What is our *need* here?"

"The same as our need there—to grow into oneness with our Origin and Destiny. Yet reaching the Center will always be a choice. Even in heaven, we must *choose* Life at the Center."

"Why would not everyone choose it?"

"Because Life at the Center involves pain—the pain of relinquishment, yielding of self, abandonment, abnegation as the Scotsman calls it. Not all are hungry enough to endure such necessities of being."

It was silent a moment. I was curious why Mount Holly's tailor had said nothing. He was one of the great elder statesmen of eighteenth century spirituality. I was eager for his wisdom.

As I had discovered with all the companions and guides I had met, he was reading my mind.

A smile came to his lips.

"Surely you haven't forgotten the importance of Quaker silences, as you used to call them?" he said.

I smiled in return. "In other words, you have been *listening.*"

"I have indeed," he rejoined. "More good is generally accomplished by listening than talking. It is one of the important contributions of our tradition to Christendom. I would offer but one brief challenge as you prepare for the next aion of your journey."

"I am eager for it," I said.

"Do you remember when it was said that certain young Christians were on fire for the Lord?" he asked.

"Of course."

"Charges of fanaticism were leveled against us Quakers in our formative years, as they were against Pentecostals and charismatics in your time."

"I was somewhat over the top myself with my enthusiasms in my youth," I said.

"All part of the growth process. Yet the term carries more truth than many realize…as you are about to discover. The Center for which you yearned is at hand. My challenge to you is this: *Embrace the fire. Abandon yourself to the Center. Follow your heart to its Home.*

Even as he spoke, a great light loomed ahead of us, a gigantic ball of fire. From it emanated profound heat such as I had never felt either here or before. It seemed that the sun itself was hurtling toward us like a flaming meteor that would surely burn up everything in its path.

"It is the fire-Center of the universe," said our Quaker elder, "the Source of God's consuming Love. You are at the threshold of the Center—the Origin and Destiny of creation."

With the words, again I was alone.

The huge sphere of light, bright and hot beyond imagining, flew toward me to engulf me. The burning sphere was encircled round about with flashing oranges and reds. But though it appeared moving at fantastic speed, it came no nearer. Whether it was ten feet away or ten million miles, I could not tell.

Its shooting flames surrounded what I now saw to be an opening, a portal of pure light in the middle of the great Sun. Yet it was a light of such infinite brightness that it appeared as a dark void of emptiness.

I wondered if I was standing before another black hole. Or was I still in the black hole I had been swept into while laying on Golgotha's cross? All about me the universe swirled in chaotic turbulence of light and blackness.

Tentatively, for it was fearsome to behold, yet eagerly, for I longed to be consumed by the Light, I moved toward it.

Some distance away to my left, I saw the man of the second cross, no first century thief but the murderer who had taken my own earthly life. I saw that he was approaching the same Sun of Fire.

He had arrived here by much different pathways of self-revelation. As I stood before an orb of Light, he stood at the edge of a chasm of infinite depth out of which rose the smoke and heat of the Great Fire. He stood at the threshold of a cliff without bottom. I sensed that he was debating how to summon the courage to plunge into the abyss before him.

A different destiny had been marked out for each of us. Yet both culminated in the same fiery Center of Light.

THIRTY-SIX

The Consuming Heart

I walked through the portal into the blazing Sun. A great silent tornado swirled about me and caught me into it. My feet flew off the ground. The hurricane of wind swept me aloft, up and up, into the maelstrom of its vortex. I was carried again into the timelessness of pure and infinite Light.

I was engulfed by the warmth of peace unimaginable. As quickly as it had begun, the windy turbulence ceased. Sound evaporated. I floated upward into a vast silence.

More words from my Quaker mentor returned to me: *Then is the soul swept into a Loving Center of ineffable sweetness, where calm and unspeakable peace steal over one. And one knows why Pascal wrote in the center of his greatest moment, the single word, "Fire." There stands the world of struggling, sinful, earth-blinded men and nations all lapped in the tender, persuading Love at the Center. There stand the saints of the ages, their hearts open to view, and lo, their hearts are our heart and their hearts are the heart of the Eternal One. In awful solemnity the Holy One is over all and in all, exquisitely loving, infinitely patient, tenderly smiling. To that Divine Life we must cling. In that Current we must bathe. In that abiding yet energizing Center we are all made one.*

Shafts of white light shot about and swirled around me. They carried no sound. Yet I felt the fingers of light probing my depths. I knew they were searching my innermost being, and that I was being perfected by God's white heat into the pure gold of sonship.

Slowly the heat of Love's cleansing mounted. I was as an unborn infant swimming helpless in my mother's womb. Yet the womb of my heavenly becoming was the Creator's heart. To him only could I cling, and only by abandoning myself to my helplessness.

I lifted my hands, even as I floated in the midst of the Light. I whispered again my heart's hunger from the garden, *I yield my all to you, my Father. I am in your hands. Be it unto me according to your Will. Perfect me as your child.*

I felt myself flying through tumultuous flames of white…higher…higher into the Infinity of Love, further up and further in… into the depths of my own Self, into the purifying light where gold was refined into its essential alloy.

Suddenly the silence was broken.

A mighty voice resounded through the Light. It was the prophet Malachi of old calling over the centuries, across the millennia, calling to all who had chosen the purifying Center and knew what it meant:

Behold, I send my messenger to prepare the way before me. For he is like a refiner's fire and like fuller's soap. He will sit as a refiner and purifier of silver. And he will purify the sons of Levi and refine them like gold and silver. And for you who fear my name, the sun of righteousness shall rise, with healing in its wings.

A great rhythmic pounding and throbbing began to echo above me. With every pulse, the whiteness rushed deeper, shooting blasts of pure energy into my depths.

The thrumming echo came from the Infinite, from heights into which no eye could see. I knew that I was entering the Source of the Light, the Heart, the Eye, the Center, ascending into the beating core of the universe, the Consuming Fire of Light

As I was gathered into it, I was inundated in Light. The throbbing continued, but without sound for I was inside it. I *felt* its reverberations in rhythm to my own heart. Light and the energy of the great Pulse absorbed me into itself.

I floated through the silence, a silence of utter bliss, for I was at the Center of the Fire at the Heart of the Light.

Words resounded over and above and through me. They were mighty echoes of truth heard not by my ears but vibrating in my inner parts as giant invisible harp strings tuned to the measure of my being. A great Voice proclaimed the truth of the ages. Time was turned inside out.

I had arrived at the moment of creation.

All around me was darkness.

I floated in the midst of empty nothingness, formless and void. Again I heard the undulating echo. The pulsating Heart was inside me because I was inside it. Nothing existed but the live Heart that was the Origin of all things.

Let there be light! thundered the silent Logos into my soul and into the soul of creation.

Whiteness exploded everywhere. Light consumed the darkness, and the darkness fled from the universe, for it could not withstand the power of the Light. I was not just at the center of the Light in my imagination—

my true being, my very essence was birthed in the moment of the mighty *Let there be.*

The Voice had not merely created Light. He had created *me*, created in his eternal mind the me that would one day come to life in the birth room I had witnessed. From infinite beginnings, he had *known* me because he had fathered me out of his own Being.

And he knew my true name known only to him. The essence of my eternal being was hidden in his heart until the day of its revelation.

THIRTY-SEVEN

From Aion to Aion

O ut of the midst of the whiteness came the figure of a Man. He was more than a man, for he had always been and would always be. He was the live beating Heart made visible to mortal eyes, and he was One with creation.

I am the Alpha! resounded the great thunder of Light. *I Am because I Am, and I will draw all creation to myself. I Am your Creator and your God and your Father, and you shall be my sons and daughters because you are my created children.*

Around me as far as the eye could see I beheld the vast teeming humanity of creation, surging and marching through the millennia from antiquity to modernity...men, women, children...old and young... rich and poor.

I saw into their hearts, for I had been given eyes to probe the mind and soul of everyone who had ever lived. I was overwhelmed by the goodness that lay in the heart of mankind. Yet I was crushed by the cruelty and greed and ambition that lay deep alongside the goodness, for it polluted the goodness by turning brother against brother and mother against daughter and son against father. And I saw meanness and depravity and neighbor spilling the blood of neighbor. And wars raged between the nations, and death seemed as if it would consume life itself because of the evil of man's cruelty and greed.

Still the nations surged through the aions, forward, ever forward, rising on the progress of the past ever to new heights, from the aion of infinite beginnings to the aion of infinite restoration.

Yet with its progress the mighty throng grew unseeing and unhearing, for the Voice that was above all and within all had grown silent. They could no longer hear the still small whispers reminding them from whence originated their life. None knew their names, or the name of the *I Am*. Sin had hardened their hearts and dulled their understanding.

When I thought I must surely despair for the plight of lost humanity, again came the great Voice. At last I saw the heads of the human tide turn and look up. Their ears began to hear. And they hearkened to the Voice at last.

I Am the Alpha and the Omega, the light and the Life, your Creator and Father, the Voice thundered. *You are my children. You must become my sons and daughters. Arise, awake, and live, and I will throw open the floodgates of heaven and pour out so much blessing that all of creation will not be able to contain it. And I will be your God, and you will be my people.*

I was walking now, moving alongside a great river, glowing red with liquid fire. The river flowed into a flaming lake of vast expanse.

I gazed into the distance from whence came the river. Worlds away, as if I were again peering backward to time's beginnings, rose the blinding red of a great

Heart of Fire, a mighty Sun like that I had walked into. It hung above the horizon and shot out flames of light. It was a live Heart, pulsating with thunderous silent echo.

Across the Heart were emblazoned four letters:
A-B-B-A.

From the Heart gushed a torrent of blood, spewing from the mortal wound of an invisible sword. But the piercing did not kill the Abba-Heart. In the throbbing agony of sacrifice, its own Life was resurrected with yet greater power. For the Heart beat with the Life that enlightens every man. As blood streamed from it, the Heart was ever renewed from out of its own death. It could not die, for it was Life itself. In its death was birthed the Life of the world.

A torrent of life-giving blood rushed forth from the Wound of Life and fueled the river of fire, and it flowed across the aions and tumbled into the lake beside me.

And I knew I was beholding the great life-birthing Heart of Father and Son, whose love together had created the world, and whose sacrifice together was redeeming it. They had redeemed me and given me power to be one with them as they were one.

Many were around me, a vast swarm of men and women. Some were throwing themselves into the river to be cleansed by sacrifice and purified by fire.

Among them I beheld the man of the second cross who had taken the thief's place beside me. Where he had come from I did not know. He had plunged into the abyss of the Fire as I had risen into the clouds in the rapture of the Light. And now the highest heights and deepest depths had met in the eternal circle of Infinite Fire and Light.

He threw himself headlong into the lake of blood. Moments later he climbed up and out of it. On his face was an expression of wonder. His body was of gold and the lake of fire could no more touch him.

Voices came from somewhere, a throng of heavenly hosts. They were chanting in unison: *And the dead were judged. Death and Hades gave up the dead that were in them. Then death and Hades were thrown into the lake of fire.*

From above came the sound of a mighty rushing fury. A meteor, huge as a moon, engulfed in fierce flames, came hurling out of the sky and plummeted with a violent explosion into the lake of fire and disappeared into its depths.

Again spoke the Voice of the Logos, ominous and mighty with command and judgment. And the Word declared: *Hell below is stirred up to meet you when you come. Your greatness is brought down to your own grave. How you have fallen from heaven, O Lucifer, son of the morning! In your heart you said, "I will ascend to heaven. I will make myself like the most High." But you shall be brought down to hell, into the depths of the Pit.*

Rain began to fall. Huge drops popped and sizzled as water met fire on the river. Yet the rain and fire were one and came from the same Source.

And I knew that God's heart felt every pain that had ever been felt in creation. He loved his creatures as the Father who had birthed them in the Light of Creation. And he loved *me*. I was his son!

Again came the echo of rhythmic pulsating over all and in all and through all. Everywhere was inside the Great Heart.

And I knew that the falling rains were God's own tears. He was suffering with his world as its pain was eradicated from the universe.

I listened. Far away—as in the heart of a silence too

full for sound, I heard a clear jubilant Scottish voice. It was singing the eternal song of creation. The words that filled my being were spoken long ago, yet were timeless and spoken anew to every generation: *Hark the herald of the Sun of Righteousness, rising with healing in its wings, the auroral wind, softly trumpeting an Approach! He comes through the solemn aionion march of the past, pregnant with eternity, drawing nigh to restore every good and lovely thing a hundredfold!*

The latter rains that fell now splashed upon my face with unspeakable comfort, for they were the refreshing rains of the dawn of a new Spring.

The throbbing of the great Heart entered my soul, for I was one with it. It vibrated in resonance with the strings of my being.

Suddenly again swirled the wind about me, drawing me into it...higher and higher...faster and faster. The light exploded into speed unfathomable. I sat on the light-tip of a bolt of lightning speeding through the universe...*inside* the universe...to the far side of its vast expanse. The sheer speed seemed it must tear me limb from limb, for I was being hurled through time and space at the speed of light itself.

A great void appeared ahead...a void of light...a great hole of black light. It drew me into its center.

Consciousness left me. Blackness engulfed me, and I fell senseless into its depths.

THIRTY-EIGHT

Tomb of Light

How and by what infinitesimal progressions I became again aware of existence, I cannot say. I lay in utter darkness, utter silence, utter aloneness.

Was I coming awake after a long sleep? It was a waking, but like no waking I had ever experienced.

How long had I lain in the blackness of oblivion? Hours, days, weeks…or an aion of ten million years? It felt like an instant. Yet in the change of waking, it seemed as though the universe had been turned inside out.

Where was I?

As feeling returned to my limbs, I realized that I was lying motionless on what felt like a slab of stone. My first thought was the harpist's bench. Yet I sensed that this was a different stone, a different time, a different place. The air was thick and still, as of an enclosed space. Yet it was somehow filled with an unexplained energy of life.

Gradual stirrings quivered in my depths. They were stirrings of new life, of a strange new *form* of life, of aionian life, the Life of the Ages. As I lay in the darkness, the well-known passage returned to my mind from its old translation:

For so greatly did God love the world that He gave His only Son, that every one who trusts in Him may not perish but may have the Life of the Ages.

By gradual degrees, something far off hinted at a thinning of the blackness. Something was approaching my chamber of isolation from afar.

Sounds gradually reached me...dissonant, chaotic, unsettling. It was the din of voices calling, crying, pleading. My heart seized me. I trembled with an awful premonition. They were cries and wails of torment!

The terrible howls of agony and lament increased...louder and louder...terrible sounds of suffering indescribable.

I lay as if for aions. All around—above, below, on every side—came moans of distress, misery, and pain...lives of unrest ruled by self, independence, and pride...souls in torment who were powerless to escape the prison of their self-doomed exile.

I suddenly realized what vision would meet my eyes if the darkness gave way. I would see the oranges and reds of terrible flames! The darkness of my sleep would be swept away by the Great Fire!

Fear possessed me with an overwhelming weight of despair.

The next moment I remembered what I had realized when I lay on the cross. I knew that I could trust him.

From somewhere now came a song, a single voice high and clear. I knew it was an angel's voice singing the message of King David's melody of hope. The words of her song resounded through the darkness, and swallowed all the cries, *If I ascend to heaven*, she sang, *you are there. If I descend into Sheol, you are there.*

I was not alone! Though I could not see him or hear him, the Lord and his Father were with me! Even in Sheol, the place of the dead, they were with me.

Words returned to me from a time and place long ago in my former life. I knew they were words given for this moment: *A great good is coming—is coming— is coming to thee. And I knew that good is always coming; though few have the simplicity and the courage to believe it.*

The Life of the Ages was approaching!

Soft distant chords now rose to accompany the angel's song. They were chords made by the invisible strings of a harp, as if from old David himself. They were joined by a second, then a third, until a great symphony of harps filled the heavens with the music of the spheres.

It was the symphony of the High Logos, the symphony of the Word, the majestic symphony of the Son.

His triumph over the forces of darkness was at hand!

THIRTY-NINE

Train of Liberation

With the symphony of the Logos reverberating in my brain, the light in the distance grew. It was not the light of the Great Fire as I had feared. It was a pinprick of pure whiteness.

It was shooting toward me. I felt a breeze on my face. The tiny ray of luminescence came rushing through the universe as a Big Bang of salvation's advance. It was millions of miles away, but was flying in my direction through space and time at the speed of light itself. It was the Light that would banish the darkness forever.

As it grew, the Light illuminated my surroundings. I saw that I was inside a small enclosed tomb of stone. As I had supposed, I was lying on a flat stone in a cavity carved into a wall of granite. Across the crypt I saw the bloodstained linen clothes in which they had wrapped the Lord's body lying on another slab like mine. The linen napkin that had bound his head was rolled up by itself. The Lord was nowhere to be seen.

I knew where I was, and that I had been in the tomb two nights and a day. But the Lord had been about his reconciling work from the very eternity of beginnings. He had been redeeming the world since the creation of the world, and would go on redeeming the world from aion to aion through all the eternity of endings. During my two days in the tomb, he had been gone for an aion, or for many aions, working the triumph of the cross throughout the eternity of the universe.

Now the Light came racing toward me. The wind from its approach rose to a tempest. Through a fiery cylinder of white it burst into the tomb from the infinite beyond. The Lord rode on the crest of light, the King of Light, though he himself *was* the Light.

A great tunnel of white spread out behind him like the tail of a comet, stretching back to creation itself. In its midst came multitudes soaring in the Lord's wake out of death and into Life.

The tears of the host had turned to rejoicing as they followed in his train. Their Deliverer had descended into the depths to deliver them. Their cries of mourning and despair were now raised in worship and praise to their Savior.

The symphony of harps was joined by a million angel voices. All the saints of heaven rejoiced with them in praise to the Savior of the universe and his Father.

Toward me out of the bowels of heaven and earth rushed the aionion march of the ages into the Light of heaven's redemption.

"My brother!" said the Lord as he saw me. "You are awake! I have been away on the Father's business. You died with me and were buried with me. Now come, we are risen. And the captives are set free and risen with us."

In the midst of the train of Light surging after the Lord I beheld my murderer-brother on a great white horse. He was leading many others by the example of his repentance. His hair flew behind him in the wind. A resplendent smile radiated from his countenance.

He saw me as he thundered by, thousands before him and thousands after him. His face brightened in childlike joy. He shouted and waved exuberantly, so happy to see me that I thought he would fall from the steed that bore him.

I laughed at his exultant greeting and waved in return.

"Praise him!" he shouted, eyes flashing. "Can you believe his great love for me! Praise to the Father!"

The light of the captive train blew into the crypt of death like a mighty wind. The boulder over the entrance of the tomb exploded from the rush of resurrection light into millions of tiny white stones of fire. On the stones were written the names of the trailing stream of men, women, and children who poured out of the tomb into the resurrection of their heavenly waking. The tiny explosions of light fluttered away into the sky on fiery white butterfly wings.

The Lord took my hand and bid me accompany him.

I stepped forth with him out of the sepulcher into the air of a glorious Easter morning. Millions poured out behind us.

All around a billion voices were singing, *Alleluia, he is risen!*

Forty

Summons

The Lord and I walked away from the tomb across an expansive field of green on a fragrant Spring morning.

"Did all that really happen?" I asked. "Or have I been dreaming?"

"Of course it happened," he replied. "It is continually happening. It is happening there every day. It is happening here as shadowy ways and means are fulfilled and perfected. Everything must be fulfilled. Salvation itself must be fulfilled."

Soon we were alone. The symphony gradually faded from my hearing until the only sound left was that of a single harp.

Nostalgic sensations, as of something remembered from long ago, filled my mind at its sound. I drifted into a reverie of pleasant memories.

In the midst of my reflections, the Lord spoke.

"Come," he said. "You are needed."

His expression had changed. I followed. No more words passed between us.

He led me toward a hazy mist. It gathered and thickened. Moments later I walked into a dense cloud of white. Coming out of it, we emerged into a churchyard. Growing out of the mist, the tombstones and building were opaque and airy. I did not at first recognize where we were. As our surroundings solidified, I knew it as the churchyard outside the Scottish village.

We walked through headstones and slabs, then through the stone wall of the church as if we were phantoms. Inside, we made our way along the aisle, empty pews on either side of us, to the pulpit. We ascended its steps. Suddenly the interior of the old church evaporated away.

I was astonished the next instant to find myself standing in my former bedroom in the house where I had lived for many years. My wife lay in bed. She was nearly motionless.

My heart seized me with untold emotions. She had aged almost beyond recognition. How could so much time have passed! She looked ancient, her hair thinning and white, her face wrinkled and drawn.

Yet her eyes were open and her expression seemed alert. She appeared content.

I glanced toward the Lord.

"Her time has come," he said tenderly.

"How long has it been…since…"

"Since you left her? Years and years. She has been a happy and productive widow."

"What happened?" I asked.

The Lord smiled. "Nothing that death will not cure. She is simply tired. Her faithful body has come to its end. She will be missed by many—more than she realizes. But she is ninety-seven. It is time. She needs you at her side. She is at peace, but a little afraid."

My heart was too full to speak. I walked across the familiar room. I sat down beside her and took her hand. I could feel it in mine. I knew she felt nothing. As I had learned, the worlds merged but did not mingle.

My wife's hand was thin and cold. It was clear that life was ebbing out of her.

I became aware that music filled the room. What else should I have expected? A harp was softly playing *Cullen Kirkyard.*

Almost the same moment, the sounds came to an end. I heard footsteps. A man entered the room. He walked to a music player of some kind I did not recognize, something new by the look of it. He pressed a button and the song began again.

I glanced toward the Lord where he stood watching.

"I seem to recognize this man," I said. "Who is he?"

"He is your son," smiled the Lord.

A gasp of astonishment left my mouth. My heart smote me with a pang of love.

My son...my dear beloved son! He had grown into a mature man, himself with graying hair. His resemblance to the earthly me was striking! I ached to run and press him to my heart!

But he was still bound to the earthly realm. I could not reach him, touch him, or in any way move his thoughts. I was powerless but to gaze upon him. How different this was from seeing his brother earlier—in an ageless heavenly body.

How I loved this boy, this youth of my memory...now become a man! I longed to see him here, too, as I had seen his brother, when I would be able to touch and kiss and embrace him!

"He and his brother and sister have been taking turns caring for their mother for some time," said the Lord. "They have developed a wonderful bond. Your son will miss his mother as much as he does you."

"He misses *me!*" I said in astonishment.

"He thinks of you every day. He calls you his life's mentor. Much that you taught him continually comes to his remembrance."

A sob burst from my mouth. Tears flowed from my eyes like a river.

As I watched, my son walked to the opposite side of the bed from where I sat. "How are you doing, Mom?" he asked. He gazed down with a smile and took her other hand. "Anything I can get you?"

"No," croaked a feeble voice. "I am very happy."

It was quiet a moment. The music of the harp continued to sound throughout the room.

"You love this song, don't you?" said our son.

My wife merely smiled and nodded.

"Ring the bell if you need anything," he said. "I'm just in the kitchen fixing some dinner. Rice and soup—hope that sounds okay."

She smiled again. What I would have given to share the simple meal with them!

He left the bedroom. We were alone again with the music. Her hand still in mine, I sat staring down at the form on the bed. My wife's eyes had closed. She was breathing easily, though in shallow breaths. She dozed off.

I waited. The Lord stood across the room in silence. His watching eyes were full of love.

My mind filled with memories of our years together. They say one's life passes before the mind's eye in an instant. In heaven, however, an *instant* might take a year...or ten years! I relished those moments at the bedside. Perhaps they did take ten years in my time, who can say.

The song was still playing. The music of *Cullen Kirkyard* wove its spell over me as well. I began to grow sleepy myself.

Time slowed.

FORTY-ONE

Another Reunion

Suddenly my senses jolted awake. An electric tingle flitted through my hand.

Had I just felt my wife's fingers twitch!

I sat up, wide awake! Her hand quivered again. There was no mistaking it. The former chill was gone. The hand resting in mine was suddenly warm.

She seemed to sense her hand enclosed by another. I felt pressure from her fingers. Her grip tightened.

My gaze, however, was glued to her face. Her eyelids began to twitch and flutter. Slowly her eyes opened.

The room grew bright. *Very* bright. She squinted and blinked, then glanced about. Finally she saw me sitting beside her. Her eyes shot wide and a gasp left her mouth. Her hand clutched mine with the strength of youth.

Her features suddenly became more pronounced, more *real*. Earth's years tumbled away. Wrinkles and lines disappeared. Her eyes brightened. Her skin took on a luminous texture. Within seconds I was gazing upon the woman I had married in the prime of her life!

Her eyes glowed as she looked about. In the first instant I think she wondered if she was dreaming. Just as quickly the intense reality hit her. She was surrounded by white light and she *knew*.

She gazed deep into my eyes and smiled. She knew where we were.

I stood and pulled her to a sitting position. She needed no help now. She rose from the bed, holding my hand with a grip of iron.

The face and body beside me were those of a strong, radiant woman of ageless beauty. Her expression was full of wonder. I could no longer see the Lord. His presence was swallowed in Light.

Hand in hand my wife and I walked across the floor and left the room together with the music of *Cullen Kirkyard* still in our ears.

The house faded into opalescence around us. We were walking down the aisle of the ancient country church. As we left the building the way the Lord and I had entered it a short while earlier—through the stone wall, not the door—my wife glanced about, then giggled with delight.

"We walked right through the wall!" she laughed.

"You are in for more surprises than that!" I said.

We emerged into the churchyard. The music of *Cullen Kirkyard* filled the air. In front of the stone slab next to the church sat a harp, its strings vibrating powerfully with the music that had called us both, each in our appointed season, awake. Breezy trees all about added their pleasurable accompaniment.

We gazed about at the many gravestones surrounding the church.

One by one, ethereal figures of white slowly came into focus, rising as out of the stones themselves. I knew that we were beholding the souls, the true personhood, of those whose earthly remnants were buried below.

Ghostly at first, their gossamer bodies took on greater and greater solidity. Around the churchyard, a dozen...now fifty...now a hundred souls emerged into heaven's resurrection. Their bodies grew strong and radiant. It was the cloud of witnesses represented by this church. The stones that held their earthly bodies faded, filmy and vaporous, into dim unreality.

Behind them and above them, a host of angels came into view. The angels and churchyard witnesses were singing the song with no name, a song called Restoration, the song whose words had not been known on the other side because they were words that could only be sung in heaven. They were the words embodied by the melodies of the harp strings whose realities could only be known here. It was music that had accompanied another soul, my wife this time, through the portal into the Life of Beyond.

As I turned back toward the church, I saw that the harp strings were no longer vibrating alone. An angel garbed in white sat on the stone. Her fingers moved with graceful rhythm up and down the strings. I wondered if she had always been playing, but my eyes had only now become able to see her.

We remained enrapt in the music of the harp and the choir and the witnesses. Gradually a path became visible on the ground before us.

As we began walking, the angel and churchyard disappeared. We found ourselves standing before the stone slab, empty now, beside the mountain and waterfalls and streams where I had come after my own waking. There stood the harp as I had come to expect, its strings vibrating in front of us. I knew that the angel was still playing, though we no longer saw her.

The mountain had grown since I had last seen it. Water pounded along its streams and falls, gushing down in torrents. It continued to grow even as we gazed upon it. Soon it became a true mountain, its streams now rivers. The pond into which it flowed was a lake of emerald green.

A great choir of angels was singing. They were singing of the Quiet Center.

The path we had taken out of the churchyard still lay at our feet. It led along a newly visible path up the mountain and along the river. As we set out to follow it, water came rushing past us on all sides. Soon we were climbing high in crisp mountain air.

Ahead the path split. There stood the Lord at the junction bathed in whiteness. I knew it was time for him to speak with my wife alone, as he had me. Her own heavenly pilgrimage awaited.

I kissed her with the affection of a brother, the joy of a friend, and the love of a husband.

I watched my beloved disappear, walking side by side with the Lord. Her heavenly journey of becoming would be as unique to her need, now that her earthly nature had fallen away, as my journey thus far had been to mine.

I took my way in the opposite direction and continued up the mountain.

I was surprised after a short distance to find my wife awaiting me. Her countenance shone with luminescence. I knew that she had been on an aionian journey as long as mine since she had left me, though it seemed that only a few minutes had passed. She was wearing a necklace sparkling with diamonds. They were the tears of her earthly life transformed into heavenly jewels with a million explosions of light inside them.

I could not wait to find out who had been some of *her* guides, and who were the men and women she had met along the way!

FORTY-TWO

The Mansions

S uddenly ahead I beheld our three children, and our grandchildren.

My wife and I ran toward them. They were beaming as we embraced. We all greeted with tears and outpourings of love. I knew them as our children and grandchildren, yet they were no longer children. They had lived their lives and arrived into heaven at the end of them. What age we were would be impossible to say. There were no outward signs of age. We beheld one another as we had become.

"Where did you all come from?" I exclaimed.

"I came from over there, Dad," said one of them. "Look—see there…between those two mountains. I had just crossed over, or crossed *through*, I should say, and had begun to climb up the slope…then I saw you and Mom!"

Behind our family reunion, a fantastic sight suddenly exploded before me. I gasped at the sight.

Away in the distance rose a multitude of glistening towers. They looked like a series of castles sitting next to each other and extending into the Mountains farther away than the extent even of my heavenly vision. It was a *city* of castles, a vast metropolis of ten thousand castles…or more! It was a fairy tale come to life.

A thrill of awe surged through me. Was I beholding the new Jerusalem, the city where God himself dwelt!

"What is that!" I exclaimed. "Just look—the towers and spires…the windows are huge…and the balconies! The views of the mountains and valleys and forests and lakes must be stunning! It's fabulous!"

I was groping for words. "What *are* they!"

"Those are the mansions!" chimed a unison of voices behind me.

I spun around. There were Bill and Sam and my parents and the Johns all laughing at my disbelieving delight to set eyes on the mansions at last.

"I want to see them!" I said excitedly. "Is that where we are going to live?"

"It is where *everyone* lives," replied a voice I did not recognize.

I turned toward it. A bearded man I had not seen before walked calmly toward me. The others parted and made way for him.

"Everyone?" I repeated.

"Of course," he answered. "Remember what the Lord said—that he was preparing mansions for each one of us. That includes you."

The man's voice and demeanor bore more signs of ageless wisdom than anyone I had yet met other than the Lord himself.

He perceived my curiosity.

"I believe you had wanted to meet me," he said with a smile. "My name is John. I wrote about the mansions long ago, as you recall. Now I have been given the privilege of escorting you into the Mountains to the mansion prepared for *you*."

FORTY-THREE

The Mountains

Hardly believing my good fortune to be walking alongside the Apostle John whom I had revered for so long, I followed excitedly. My heart gushed with gratitude.

"I can't thank you enough," I said, "for setting down in such detail the Lord's conversation with you and the others that last night you were together in the upper room."

"It was the Spirit who brought it to my remembrance, and imbued it with power," said John with a quiet smile. "I could never have remembered everything on my own."

"I am so grateful for that entire passage, and the Lord's prayer at the end of it," I went on. "It helped me so many times. To my mind it represented the culmination of the gospel. I considered it the most important passage in the New Testament."

John smiled again. His expression hinted at that of an older and wiser elder listening to the babblings of youth. As I was discovering, there were levels of wisdom and maturity even in heaven. Alongside the Lord's youngest disciple and earthly cousin, I was still a babe of eternity. Yet his reply was kind, gracious, and as tender as his voice.

"We do not speak of *most* important things here," he said. "Truth is truth. All truth is important because God's being lies at the heart of it. I wrote what the Spirit gave me to write. That is all. I am deeply pleased that it ministered to your heart, and to your growing awareness of the Lord's command to love."

He smiled, almost nostalgically as he recalled his own growth, perhaps in heaven as well as on earth.

"His words were equally powerful in my own life," he went on. "Your quest and mine were the same. It is the quest of all God's sons and daughters—to know the Son and the Father through the revelation of the Spirit."

As we went, my wife was still at my side. Our sons and my father and my grandfather on my mother's side and both of the other Johns and my father-in-law and Bill and Sam and Sam's wife and my two Quaker mentors were clustering about us. They were as eager to hear the apostle's words as I was.

"Besides," added John, chuckling as if remembering an inside joke, "not everyone would agree with you about the relative importance of that passage."

As he spoke, he glanced around. I detected a brief wink and grin at one of his two namesakes. Calvin returned his look with a smile.

"There are *some*," the apostle went on with fun in his tone, "not to mention any names of course, who happen to think brother Paul's writings the most important. I'm sure you will enjoy talking over such things with Paul and the others."

"I am eagerly looking forward to it!" I said.

"You will have your chance soon enough. A few of

us get together for the most fascinating discussions. I'm not able to participate as often as I like. We are so busy. There's just so much to do! I have more demands on my time than ever. But I plan to make it next time. With you joining us, it promises to be a spirited discussion. I'm sure you will bring valuable new insights to the group.—You'll be there, won't you, John?" he added, turning again to the other John.

"Wouldn't miss it," replied Calvin.

"I would be privileged merely to listen," I said. When you say a few...I would think *everyone* would want to be part of it."

"People have their own interests, even here. It is usually only a few thousand, ten at the most. Paul tells me there are some passages he is eager to discuss with you."

"Don't most come to listen to him, or you or Peter or one of the other disciples?" I said. "I can't imagine I could add much of interest."

"You would be amazed," rejoined John. "Now that God's High Logos Truth is revealed, the insights from *everyone* are breathtaking. Actually, those of us who have been here longest generally say very little. We enjoy simply listening."

Again he glanced back, this time catching the eye of his Quaker namesake.

"Or as my brother often reminds us by his countenance," he added, "we relish in the silences."

The apostle turned to my wife.

"And what about you?" he asked. "Will you join us as well?"

"I don't know," she replied. "I'm interested, of course. But I don't know that I am *quite* so eager to meet Paul. I struggled with his teachings about women."

John roared with laughter.

"Yes, that comes up quite often around here! In Paul's defense, I will tell you from one who knows him intimately that he has changed many of his views. I assure you that you will find him delightful."

My wife nodded appreciatively.

"As you might suspect, we don't make much of gender here," John went on. "All are one. That said, however, Paul is very humble around women. He regrets some of his former statements. Therefore, he is now anxious to learn from *them*."

"Still, theological discussions aren't really my cup of tea," said my wife. "As I said—all that is interesting, but theology seems like a waste of time to me. I'm more anxious to sing in the choir."

"That's wonderful," rejoined John. "Then you've probably spoken with Sam already. He leads several choirs."

"I also hope to learn to play the harp."

"Then we will definitely need to get you together with Mary, the Lord's mother. She is one of those who teach new arrivals. She also has the most delightful voice. When she and the women get together, singing to the accompaniment of the harp choir, sometimes with the angels...the music is positively rapturous."

"I can't wait to sing with them! Do you think they can use another alto?"

John smiled. "I am sure of it," he replied.

FORTY-FOUR

The Processional

W e continued onward and upward. We were in high mountains now. I was reminded of walking through the highest of the Colorado Rockies and the Swiss Alps, with the best of both all about us. We made our way through verdant meadows and fields nestled among high peaks between forested groves. Sounds of water came from everywhere—trickling brooks and mighty rivers and waterfalls plunging down from high above.

Occasionally we ran splashing and laughing through a mountain stream. Ten minutes later a sturdy footbridge might lead us across a rocky gorge so close to a spectacular and turbulent waterfall that the spray billowed up and surrounded us in its refreshing mist.

The air was so crisp, yet unlike the air of earth. The higher we climbed the *easier* it became to breathe. Every breath filled the lungs with the Source of Life itself, of which earthly oxygen, as all earthly types, was but a shadow of heaven's reality.

When we were not crossing streams and canyons,

below our feet spread the most luxuriant carpet of grass interwoven with every color of alpine wildflower imaginable. Its millions of blossoms were as tiny as the blades of grass—violets, edelweiss, columbine, poppies, daisies, lavender, and innumerable others only a few of which I had ever seen.

Indefinable aromas—cleansing, rich, alluring, satisfying, and joyfully nostalgic—rose from the flowery carpet and filled the air with yet more life. They entered the senses like fragrance-food for the soul. As if energized by the richness of the air, hummingbirds and other winged creatures flitted about, while above eagles, owls, and hawks soared in great circles welcoming us to their lofty regions. I was reminded of the lion and the lamb. Here also were the eagle and the hummingbird making sport in the breezes together. I imagined their beaks, so distinctively different, shaped in smiles as they flew among us.

Many joined us as we went. They came along in ones and twos and threes, then in companies of tens and fifties and hundreds, moving in the same direction. Before long it was a grand procession. We were walking purposefully in rhythm to faint music now audible in the distance.

Faces continually glanced toward us as we went, smiling and happy. It was clear that some great celebration was at hand and they had been invited to it. We were being drawn, beckoned, led toward something that I could not yet imagine.

Gradually the music became stronger. We felt it swirling around us like a soft breeze; we inhaled it as it arose from the lush carpet of flowers beneath our feet. It began to reverberate from the mountains surrounding us, as if in fulfillment of Isaiah's prophecy. If they had not exactly broken forth in singing, the mountains and hills had broken forth in *music*. Some great symphony of celestial violins and violas and cellos and every imaginable kind of wind instrument and French horns and trombones with, of course, innumerable harps, was somewhere in the mountains or beyond. Thousands of musicians—angels perhaps—were playing the majestic music of a grand processional and we were being drawn inward and upward by it.

Just as our colorful pathway contained all the flowers of earth and more, so also the processional combined the greatest compositions that the musicians of earth had been capable of producing, and far *more* than they had imagined, now elevated to become the grand processional of heaven. I heard faintly familiar strains from Mendelssohn and Brahms, Elgar and Mozart, and Handel and Pachelbel all intermingling together. There even came moments—I had to laugh at the wonderful incongruity of it!—when I detected hints of McCartney and Dylan, Cash and Orbison, woven among them.

Children were running among us, picking the flowers out of the grass and dancing about. I wondered if these innocent cherubs were those who had been taken out of the earth as infants, or even before their birth, and were now enjoying the rare privilege of growing into their eternal personhood in heaven. What an incredible thing to be a child in heaven! And yet we were all becoming heaven's children! The angelic youngsters were full of joy, tossing the flowers into the air and strewing the path before me with thousands of tiny petals.

"It looks like we have come upon a wedding," I said to the apostle, who was still beside me. "Or perhaps another huge family reunion!" I added, laughing.

John laughed. "You are not far wrong!" he said.

"Actually, it is both."

"Why is everyone staring at *me* and throwing flowers in front of me?"

"Because it *your* welcome home party!"

"Mine!"

"You didn't think we would miss the opportunity to celebrate, did you? You are the guest of honor. It is your wedding."

"All this lavish preparation . . . for me!"

"These people, these children, these saints of God are here to celebrate with you."

I could only stare at him in wonder.

"It is a feast in your honor," John added, "the Lord's wedding banquet, and the great reunion of the Father's family."

"How did all these people know I was coming? I don't recognize half of them. What am I saying—I don't recognize a millionth of them!"

John laughed again.

"It is for you . . . but not *only* for you," he said. "It is continually in progress because the celebrants increase daily. The wedding feast is an integral part of life in the mansions. Like everything here, it is for *everyone*."

I had no time to ponder his words.

FORTY-FIVE

A Woman and Her Chalice

A̲ll at once speeding toward the processional from some gap through the hills to our right, I saw a carriage appointed almost entirely in white. It was racing along pulled not by horses but by two huge white fluffy dogs the size of Shetland ponies. I had no idea what was their pedigree. They appeared to be some combination of St. Bernard, Giant Samoyed, Great Pyrenees, or even South Russian Ovcharka—huge, gleeful, and full of the vibrant energy so unique to their species. They were dogs one would see nowhere but in heaven. In the carriage sat a woman resplendently attired in robes of white and red and purple. She was obviously of royal lineage. On her head sat a crown of pure gold. I took her for a princess.

Suddenly a great noisy commotion erupted that nothing, even after all I had seen and heard, could have prepared me for.

From out of the Mountains and mansions above us came streaming down toward the princess and her magnificent charges a veritable multitude of creatures of every imaginable size and shape and color—dogs, cats, horses, giraffes, moose, deer, chipmunks, tigers, mice, skunks, sheep, rabbits, beaver, pigs, goats, squirrels, hippopotamuses, raccoons, elephants, foxes, zebras, elk, cows, buffalo, and all manner of lumbering bears from black to white…and every other kind of beast. A contingent of turtles hurried to keep up. I wondered if Noah's Ark had just landed and opened its doors! The cacophony of barks, squeals, brays, bleats, squawks, yelps, and roars was so riotous I could only laugh at the sight.

To the thundering base-drum cadence of the elephants' footfall, the creature-horde made straight for their mistress and her two great white dogs, trying to welcome them with as much noise as they could muster. In the midst of the din, I began to detect hints of strange melodies and harmonies. I knew that the animals, like the angels, were making a symphony of praise all their own. If the lion and the lamb in the midst of the throng were not exactly lying down together, they were certainly running and cavorting and roaring and bleating together, fully aware of the symbolism of their frolicking animal friendship.

Before the bounding tumultuous animal throng reached them, however, the princess reined in.

I had not noticed him before. Beside the road sat a miserable-looking man holding a can and begging for whatever pennies came his way. He was a pitiful wretch clothed in rags, gaunt and emaciated. Cancerous sores covered his body. Even from where I stood, the foul stench of his diseased body stung my eyes.

Stunned as I watched, I beheld as the woman got down out of her seat and knelt beside him. On the surrounding hillsides, the multitude of animals ceased their madcap rush. A dust cloud rose as they jostled and bumped to a stop. Silence descended. Every creature appeared to bow its head reverently.

From her carriage, the woman took a chalice of pure gold. With one hand she held it to the man's lips. He drank deeply. With her other hand she took a corner of her white robe and wiped at his eyes and face. She then bent down and kissed his cheeks and forehead. Setting aside the chalice, she rose and extended her hand. Feebly he reached up and took it. She helped the man to his feet, then invited him into her carriage to sit beside her.

At last they were settled.

"To the feast!" she shouted.

Her two royal canines bounded into motion again with their guest.

As they flew away up the hill, the horde of creatures again exploded into frantic motion, scampering, frolicking, romping, and leaping after them. As they went, the woman turned. Her gaze pierced mine, and she smiled.

I saw into her eyes, and I knew her! It was just as the Lord had promised. She was the stooped old woman in the supermarket, and the prayer lady of the lake. She might have been the girl with the kittens as well. That would explain her affection for heaven's creature population, and theirs for her. But I couldn't be sure. The man she now bore to the Marriage Supper of the Lamb was none other than he whom I had seen shove her aside in the store.

"The very same," said John at my side, knowing what I was thinking. "She will now be used in his salvation."

As we continued on our way, my mentor of the Center came up beside me.

"Don't forget our date to visit Cain's wife," he said. "Now that you are in the Mountains, I see no reason to postpone it.

"Sure," I laughed. "At least I guess so. I'm not sure what's on the agenda."

"Actually, you're going to be rather busy for the rest of the day . . . or it may be for several days," he said with a smile. "Perhaps after that will work for you."

"After what everyone has said, I am really looking forward to seeing Paul too," I added. "I'd rather not wait for that meeting John was talking about. It sounds like it would be hard to get him alone."

My father, who was walking beside us, now spoke. "We'll pay him a visit soon as well," he said. "I've already arranged it with him."

"You talked to Paul!"

My father nodded with a peaceful smile.

"That's great, then!" I said. "Where does he live? Where is *his* mansion?"

"On the other side of the Mountains."

"How long will it take us to get there?"

"Not long. A few minutes. It's close by."

"I guess Bill was right," I laughed. "In heaven everyone is neighbors with everyone."

FORTY-SIX

Heaven's Feast

The processional engulfed us again and we continued on. Gradually the mountains opened before us.

Between two lofty peaks ahead I beheld a magnificent sight. A palace of gigantic dimensions rose out of the mountains as if it had literally grown out of the granite of itself. It towered over the tallest peaks, a crowning centerpiece among the vast array of mansions I had seen earlier. The heavenly dwellings spread out from the palace in every direction, as though they had been birthed out of its grandeur.

Indeed, the shape of the heavenly chalet or pavilion or palatial manor—words of attempted description become meaningless!—reminded me of a crown, as if it were the topmost jewel set with rejoicing upon the very heights of heaven. The design was like nothing on earth, for it was *perfect*. The shape and artistry embodied all the architectural genius of earth, glorified now into its eternal Ideal.

It was solid and real, yet was a *living* and *growing* structure, for Life was within it. Spires and turrets and domes of blue and gold and glistening white—bordered with diamonds and rubies and sapphires and precious stones—reflected with dazzling brightness, and sparkled with all the colors of the rainbow.

What to call it! A majestic castle...a citadel...a temple...a royal mansion-city set on heaven's hill.

Perhaps . . . a Church.

Surely I had come face to face with the living Temple that was *the* Church, alive because it had been built of live souls who were becoming the sons and daughters of God.

Waterfalls and rivers and ponds and gardens and woodlands extended out and away from the elegant pinnacle of the heavenly City on all sides, with innumerable paths and walkways leading to the sparkling mansions beyond.

I knew that I was approaching the heavenly Jerusalem, with this great Temple at the heart of it surrounded by the dwelling places that had been prepared for God's saints, the eternal home of all mankind.

The procession moved toward it, and I was at its center. Great Sempervirens and Sequoias formed seven pillars—live, growing pillars—of the entryway to the immense Palace. Their branches and boughs spread in thick profusion in all directions and became the supporting beams of an ornate domed and towered roof that extended higher than the eye could see.

As we approached, the symphony around us increased. Louder and louder it rose in magnificent crescendo. The moment I stepped through the massive redwood columns, thunder as from a thousand kettledrums shook the ground beneath my feet and filled my body with its reverberations.

Though the sound was too high and too loud to detect the Voice in its midst, somehow I knew that the thunder had spoken *my* name, announcing my entry into the Marriage Feast of the Lamb.

I continued inside. The instant I crossed the threshold, the music of the processional evaporated away. The echo of thunder slowly faded. Profound silence descended as if throughout all heaven.

I looked about. If this temple-mansion was indeed a *Church*, I found myself in no sanctuary of pulpits and pews, but rather in a magnificent and elegantly appointed banquet hall that seemed to go on forever . . . away and up and out in every direction without end. The inside of this palace was larger than the outside!

Tables as far as the eye could see—and *beyond*, for this was the realm of the infinite glorified Beyond— extended for miles, spread with white linen woven on the looms of angels. The tables overflowed with food and wine and drinks that cannot even be imagined, with gold and silver goblets foaming and steaming and frothing. Every inch was exquisitely lovely, the colors fiery and intense. I was beholding food and drink that had been grown, produced, created, made, and baked in heaven to sustain our heavenly beings. Dazzling fruits and vegetables and spices and cheeses and herbs and breads and cakes and puddings were laid out everywhere. Grapes the size of apples, berries as big as a fist, filled crystal bowls. Trays of gold and silver were piled with a multitude of growing edible delights that God had reserved for heaven—all inviting new revelations, giving off aromas and hinting at pleasures never before enjoyed by human senses.

Guests were seated—thousands, perhaps millions— all beaming. Every set of smiling eyes was looking at *me* to welcome me!

Still silence reigned. Amid their smiles was a universal expression of expectation. They were waiting.

Now out of the silence emerged a strong, single voice singing the Aeonian Anthem, the Song of the Ages. In what language the great Melody of Redemption filled the hall, I could not say. All heard and all understood. Every note of its timeless euphony was palpable, pure, lovely beyond description, and filled with power. It went into my ears as if I were drinking the sound, breathing the sound. The hearing of the One Song, the Song of Unity, the Hymn of Reconciliation, swept all my senses up into it. The taste of the music flowed into my head like the wine and delectable fig cakes of Israel's man of wisdom. The aroma of the melody wafted through me as if I had been transported into the midst of a rose garden. Every nerve of my body was alive. The Psalm of Eternity entered into my very being.

I knew who was singing, for he was among us, and he was drawing near. The Singer was Christ Jesus himself, the Lord, the Son, the Eternal Brother and Bridegroom of mankind singing in welcome to his Bride.

As I watched him come, suddenly I realized that I was wrapped in a robe of purest white.

The Lord was singing to me, for he had been waiting for me . . . for us all! The Church was his Bride and he was our Beloved Groom, Brother, Savior, Lord, and Friend. His eyes probed mine, piercing to the depths. He smiled, and I knew I was one with the Bridegroom of Creation. Then he turned and was singing to others as he had to me.

"And the ceremony?" I said to John beside me, "— the wedding itself? When will it take place?"

"It took place long ago," he replied. "He has been our Bridegroom from the dawn of time. We now celebrate the eternal reality that has always been. So come, my brother—enter into the Marriage Feast with rejoicing!"

Voices of praise now rose to join the Wedding Song of the Son. They came from everywhere. I beheld thousands, millions of worshipping saints with me all clad in lustrous white.

And I knew, as John had said, that every one present was a guest of honor. We were celebrating together the marriage of the Bridegroom to his Bride. We were his Chosen, united and one with each other and him, without spot, wrinkle, or blemish.

Amid the food were folded hand-towels of humble weave and homespun linen which looked out of place amid the finery around us everywhere. Beside them sat equally humble clay basins, unpainted, unglazed, and unadorned.

Over all and through all and above all, the One Song continued.

As I made my way toward the tables, I knew that the Feast had been in progress for aions, for it was always beginning anew in every heart. It was a celebration that continually rejoiced as each new soul entered into the family of God, and would continue doing so until the end of eternity.

Multitudes sat at the ornately appointed tables, while others reclined on great cushions, visiting, laughing, eating, drinking, talking, and sharing memories as they ate and drank. Angels bustled among us, talking and laughing and sharing stories from their lives, so very different from ours. They were as full of questions about us as we were about them!

Set within the walls surrounding us were shadow boxes depicting scenes from the lives of God's people, pivotal turning points from their days on earth. They were living portrayals that came alive before the eyes, reminders of decisive moments and choices that had contributed toward eternal growth. There were no tears, no guilt, no reminders of former failings. All such had been dealt with before arriving at the Feast. Only invisible victories were now celebrated. Around the room as the feast continued, the images attracted great attention. Many clustered about watching, breaking out cheering and with applause at every act of kindness, forgiveness, or self-denial from lives that had gone before.

Friends new and old greeted me with joy. I sought out many whom I wanted to meet as well, from saints and prophets and apostles of old—especially the angels Michael and Gabriel—to acquaintances from the City of Gratitude. We embraced for minutes or hours, without need of words. Each time I stepped back from a sister or brother of the heavenly childship I knew that we had been in conversation for an aion. Our hearts had flowed together, and we knew as we were known.

The Feast went on and on, for months, for years, for all of Eternity. I continued hearing occasional faint ripples of thunder, and I knew the names of new arrivals were continually being announced.

As I ate I savored every bite as it entered into me, tingling and full of life. The wine and Spirit-nectar enlivened every fiber of my senses and filled me with knowledge of eternal mysteries. Though we now possessed incorruptible bodies, the food and drink yet penetrated into every pore. I felt as though I were imbibing palpable light. As it entered into my depths, vast reservoirs were opened of thought, taste, touch, smell, sight, and knowing—all raised and glorified into one.

Amid the throng a Man was moving among us. As he came to each he offered drink from a chalice in his hand, full and ever-renewing. It was the Lord, the Son, the Host of the Feast, offering not mere sips of wine but offering himself as the very Life of Heaven.

As his eyes again met mine, I knew him and he knew me. His life flowed in me and through me, and his smile of Love seared my eyes with light and exploded into my heart with joy.

He met each one as he met me. All eternity lay before him and behind him to serve. Though he was the reason for the Feast, he was also the Servant-Groom, whose will it was to do his Father's will, to serve and give his life for his brethren.

FORTY-SEVEN

Eternal Supper of Servanthood

When all had partaken, the Lord came among us again, offering each one from a warm fragrant loaf in his hands.

He was inviting us to participate in the Eternal Now of that timeless supper by which he had prepared his disciples for his death. It had, in fact, been no "last" supper, but was in reality the *first* birthing fellowship-meal of a New Covenant feast which had been in progress ever since. It was an eternally renewing feast, inaugurated and given power that night in the Upper Room in Old Jerusalem, forever now glorified in the New Jerusalem. The simple supper of old had become the glorious Wedding Feast of heaven.

And as that ancient First Supper had been the type and perfection of all suppers and feasts and celebrations to follow, the Lord now set aside the bread and wine.

He bent to his knees, smiled up to a great hulking man seated before him, then took a towel and poured water into a basin, and began to wash the man's feet.

"Lord, do you wash my feet?" he said, returning the Lord's smile.

Suddenly I knew that Peter himself was in our midst, and that he and the Lord were showing us the life of heaven.

"What I am doing," rejoined the Lord, "you did not understand then, but you understand now, and thus you are clean and whole."

Next he turned to me, with towel in hand, and smiled. I bowed my head and closed my eyes. I felt the Lord's humble ministrations as he washed and dried my feet. My body trembled with warmth at the touch of his fingers.

He moved on from one to another to another through the great hall.

At last he stood and spoke. His voice was soft—the still small voice of the Ages—yet reverberated throughout his kingly Palace:

I have set you an example, he said, *that you should do as I have done. As I have washed your feet, you are also to wash one another's feet. If you know these things, blessed are you if you do them. For to serve is the will of the Father. To serve is the life of Heaven.*

Instantly and without hesitation, thousands rose from their chairs, tables, and cushions. Taking the homespun linen towels and clay basins that had been supplied, all began to wash and dry their neighbors' feet. Then those who had ministered allowed themselves likewise to be ministered unto.

Though our feet were already clean, we all in turn— taking now the part of servant, now the part of being served—rejoiced in re-enacting the symbolic fulfillment of the Lord's life on earth, now glorified and sanctified as the Life of heaven: service and ministry one to another. Low murmurs of gratitude and thanksgiving spread among us, and went on for hours, even as the feast continued as well.

I found myself washing Peter's feet, then John's. My heart was humbled to participate in the timeless sacrifice with these great men in the Spirit. Yet I knew they rejoiced to serve, for they had learned well from their Master. Then I washed the feet of my father and mother and my wife and those of my children, and likewise was served by them in turn.

The Wedding Feast was complete. My heart rejoiced, and I was glad.

FORTY-EIGHT

Stairway to Heaven's Throne

Music had begun again, the great Symphony was playing anew.

I recognized it, not as a processional now but as a triumphant recessional. It was time for me to leave the Palace of the Wedding Feast.

The music rose as a Benediction of things that had been, yet was filled with ever renewing Beginnings of all that was to come. Eternity was turned inside out from Beginnings to Endings and to Beginnings again. The Wedding was complete, yet the marriage of Christ and his Bride—and the servanthood of its essential Life—would continue as the living reality of Eternity.

As I left through the far end of the Palace, I saw that it was now a gigantic open-air pavilion without walls. People were coming and going from all sides, flowing in and out and walking to and from the mansions, and I knew that the celebration would go on and on as an ever-renewing Feast.

I was with my family and loved ones again, and we left the Pavilion of the Feast to continue our eternal journey. We were walking yet higher, into the very blue of heaven itself.

Around us rose a great confluence of languages. Voices of praise roared like a chorus of celestial Narnian lions, then whispered soft as the breath of a baby angel. I heard every tongue of the earth and tongues that were not of the earth.

The eternal symphony rose into the vault above, as if the air itself was imbued with the soul of heaven's song. We were entering into the heart of the music, and every knee was bowed in veneration and adoration.

And we worshipped him and praised the God of heaven, of earth, of things under the earth, and of all the universe.

Every voice, with ours, each in his own tongue, loudly proclaimed:

Jesus Christ is Lord, to the glory of God the Father!

Fresh breezes of Spring, fragrant with eternal newness of life, wafted their secrets to the ends of the universe. Blue spread endlessly above. Green rolled away from our feet.

Again I found myself among peaks and forests, valleys and meadows, brooks and lakes, spreading all about us. Waterfalls and rivers and streams flowed down steep slopes. They all stretched away forever. The landscape was *larger* and more *real* and beautiful than anything that had ever been or ever could be anywhere but in heaven.

And now at last one peak rose higher than all the rest. A mighty river flowed from its heights above, plunging through the mountains, its banks filled to overflowing with translucent emerald green.

As we walked up the slopes toward the fountainhead of the crystalline river, from every direction vast multitudes joined us. They were ascending the Mountains from everywhere. Truth was no longer fragmented into the divisions of men but was one, as all things were one, and the Man of Light, the Lord of Salvation, Jesus Christ the Son of God, was hailed and praised as the embodiment of every truth. Every voice blended in melodious praise, every face glowing with joy.

The song from the multitude rose into the heavens and caught up into it all the music that had been written and all the music that had been sung and all the music that had even been imagined. Some wept, others danced. All were wide-eyed with wonder at the glory of it, for it was at once the music of the heart and the music of the spheres. It was all the music that had ever been, culminating in the song of the One who sat on the throne.

Swarms of millions—or was it billions!—came from many directions. All were ageless because the age of the aions had entered into us. We were now of the Age of the Ages.

We were making our way up the highest Mountain, and toward what I now saw to be a great stairway beside the emerald river. From every direction, emanating out of the air itself, resounded the music of harps. We were on our way to be given the names that had been in God's heart for each of us from the beginning of creation.

I saw a figure appear at the top of the stairway. He began descending toward us. He was tall, radiant, powerful, tender, compassionate, forgiving, ageless, for he was the Almighty, the Ancient of Days.

It is the Father, I heard a Voice say. I glanced beside me. A translucent figure of white was walking with me. And I knew the Spirit was speaking into my heart. *He is coming to welcome you into the fullness of your sonship.*

I trembled with anticipation and joy.

As he came slowly down the stairs, though the light of life shown from his eyes, the blinding light I had seen emanating from the Lord, and the whiteness of the Spirit's ethereal form, had dissipated into the pure air of heaven's clarity. No obscuring light stood between himself and his children. The image of the Father was visible and real. There was no barrier to prevent his sons and daughters at last from beholding him exactly as he was. The season when man could not look upon his face was no more. Now his sons and daughters must look upon his face, that they might live!

I did look upon it. And I beheld the face of Infinite Love, the face of perfect Fatherhood.

I wept as he came toward me, his arms outstretched. On his face was a great and welcoming smile. As we embraced, he spoke my new name. It was the name he had prepared for me since before the foundation of the world, and whose reality he had been preparing me to receive since he first envisioned me in his heart of love

And I heard singing, millions upon millions of voices in unison. It was the Anthem of the angels and the animals and those at the Feast and all the sons and daughters of God, and all heaven, for I was one of them, and my own voice rose in praise with the rest.

And we were singing, *Now the dwelling of God is with men, and they will be his people, and God himself will be their God. He will wipe every tear from their eyes. There will be no more death or mourning forever, for the aion of eternity has come.*